The Cannibal Gardener

Joe Pawlowski

Glint Media

NEWHOPE, MINNESOTA

Also by Joe Pawlowski

The Watchful Dead
Dark House of Dream
The Vermilion Book of the Macabre

Joe Pawlowski/Glint Media
New Hope, Minnesota
www.joepawlowskiauthor.com

Publisher's Note: This is a work of fiction. Names, characters, places, and incidents are a product of the author's imagination. Locales and public names are sometimes used for atmospheric purposes. Any resemblance to actual people, living or dead, or to businesses, companies, events, institutions, or locales is completely coincidental.

Book Layout © 2017 BookDesignTemplates.com
Book Cover by SelfPubBookCovers.com/lizandrashaw

The Cannibal Gardener/ Joe Pawlowski -- 1st ed.
ISBN 978-1-7336108-6-5

To Shirley Jackson, Ramsey Campbell and Joyce Carol Oates, for their captivating brands of strangeness, and to my pulp-writer heroes Lester Dent, Robert E. Howard and H.P. Lovecraft. Doc rocks, Conan is king, and Cthulhu rules.

Early in the morning before the children were awake, she was already up, and when she saw both of them sleeping and looking so pretty, with their plump red cheeks, she muttered to herself, "That will be a dainty mouthful!"

—JACOB AND WILHELM GRIMM, "HANSEL AND GRETHEL"

Contents

> Chapter One

The ways of our people came from a time when the world was young, when the air was fresh and crisp, and the sky and the sea were the color of blue jacarandas in the light of dawn. We lived in an island jungle where coconuts and bananas were plentiful, and the fish leapt at the chance to be caught in our nets. We ate tannin-leached acorns and pithed sago palms, yams and taro, bitter oranges and breadfruit. Every evening we had a feast around a bonfire on the sandy shore, lasting until the moon and the stars lit the night."

She paused, a look of reminiscence enlivening the deep wrinkles and drawn contours of her face as if recalling, firsthand, these days thousands of years ago.

"Drink your coffee, Grandam, before it gets cold."

He held the cup to her lips and she sipped. Focus returned to her eyes.

"Back then, we lived in huge huts on piles. The whole community lived together in four shelters connected by bamboo walkways. Every member had a role to play. Weavers, potters, fishers, cooks. There was no government, no chiefs. Everyone just knew what to do and did it. We functioned with one mind, as one organism. Nothing that needed doing went undone."

He had heard these stories before, many times. But he never tired of watching her tell them. Some essence within her always came alive in the telling.

"Of course when threatened we all became warriors." She mumbled something more, and he could see she was getting tired.

"Why don't you take a nap, Grandam? I'll get a blanket."

"Yes, of course. A little nap."

She closed her eyes.

He left the room, pulled the comforter from her bed, and returned to tuck it around her in the rocking chair. She had already nodded off. *No one sleeps like the old*, he thought. *So peaceful. So relieved to be free of the pressures of life; of planning and scheming and all manner of discursive thinking.*

He supposed that after ninety years, the voice in her head had become quite monotonous.

The apartment was small, but the living room had a large window that flooded in light, and there were enough warm touches to make the place comfortable. A loveseat with a hand-woven throw faced a portable television on a stand. A print of a Gauguin landscape dominated one wall: mountains vibrant with electric colors. There were doilies, knickknacks, a candy dish on a coffee table. There were unlit candles with pictures of saints curving around their edges, a writing desk with a computer on it, a straight-back chair with a cushioned seat. And in the corner near the air conditioner, a Tiffany floor lamp.

And, of course, plants were everywhere, plants suspended from the ceiling by macramé slings or emerging from naked pots on flat surfaces: ferns, orchids, ponytail palms, devil's ivy, jade and zebra plants. Each nourished with loving care down to the last detail. Impossibly perfect plants that a visitor might initially take to be artificial, if visitors were ever allowed in the apartment.

In the background, the coffeemaker gurgled in a way that always made him think of a giant sea turtle choking down a mouthful of seaweed.

She snored softly now. Edmund St. Claire went to the computer desk, sat in the straight-back chair and began to type.

He went to the TOR browser, inserted a special USB drive for Tails, and, like that, he was in, browsing the dark underbelly of the internet. His playground.

His first stop was a site that featured graphic photos of atrocities: Nazi butchery, police crime scenes, battlefield carnage. He perused with interest. Someone on this site had posted a link to a collection of horrendous highway fatalities, not strictly atrocities but of interest to site visitors nonetheless. He followed the link and browsed the impressive compilation for a half-hour or so, then moved to another site, this one focusing on methods of torture. Images of death and anguish flickered hypnotically before his eyes.

Finally, he entered the Forlorn Flesh Fetishist, the only dark site on which he posted, signed in as Raoul153 and scrolled through his messages. Most were old ones that he saved to revisit. But one was new.

From Vlad98 in Tennessee, a web designer: "Your offer tempts me, Raoul. When I picture it, I see myself lying on a silver tray in a gravy of my own juices, my bare skin waiting for your knife's delicate slice. I feel its keen caress, and the piercing tines of your fork as you raise a tender portion of me to your lips, to your teeth. My flavors dance in your mouth, and you wash me down with a goblet of my blood. Could there be a more exquisite end?"

Edmund grinned.

Closing the message, he went next to the news feed and scrolled through the posts. Photos mostly of men but not exclusively. Smooth-skinned adolescents and adults, some in masks, some with blurred-out faces. They appeared at dinner tables, in bedrooms, in suburban living rooms, striking sinister poses straight out of 1950s horror movies. Wannabes, by and large, holding up Photoshopped heads, relishing bloody slabs of meat. Some of the pictures he had seen before on other websites: corpses missing limbs, and so on.

He paused on a photo of a nude woman. She held a whip that appeared to be formed from a human spine. Manic streaks of mascara accented the haunting quality of her eyes. Blood ran from her mouth, down her chin, catching on her brown areolas and leaving splash marks on her belly's soft paunch. Behind her on the wall was a pentagram fashioned from the mounted head of a goat, a print of Francesco Goya's *Saturn Devouring His Son*, and an altar covered in Santería and Vodun charms (including an authentic-looking skull). In her other hand, she offered a framed print of an old peasant woman with jagged teeth.

The poster's handle was MsBathory. He stared at her, breathless, the blood churning in his lower regions.

Just like that, she had bound him in her spell.

He wanted to message her but was lost for words.

"Edmund?"

Grandam was awake from her nap. How long had he been tripping through cyberspace? He glanced at the clock on his screen. 11:16 a.m.

"Don't you work this afternoon?" she asked.

Edmund exited the site, exited the dark web. "It's alright, Grandam. I've plenty of time."

He pulled out the USB drive and returned it to his pocket. Then he walked the brief, narrow hall to the bathroom. Before departing for work, he needed to attend to the urgency stirring in his loins.

MsBathory, he thought wistfully, closing and locking the bathroom door.

***

One of Denise Nils' fondest memories was of her First Communion.

She recalled rising from the rigid pew in her new white veil, white lace dress, and white cloth gloves, and entering a moving line of seven-, eight- and nine-year-olds, likewise garbed in white. Of course, the boys only wore white shirts, but from her vantage point as an awestruck second-grader, all she saw was a row of dazzling, virginal white leading to the priest and altar boys near the front of the church.

The innocents filed with heads bowed and hands held together— some hands draped in rosary beads—striding straight and attentive like slow-marching soldiers, the fabric of their dresses and trousers rustling amid organ music and resounding choruses of "Welcome, welcome, welcome, Jesus." Down the carpeted aisle, into the fragrant aroma of resinous copal incense.

As she neared the head of the line, the priest repeated the magic words, "The body of Christ," and she imagined the wafers transforming into something otherworldly in the mouths of the communicants.

Over the altar hung the Son of God from a wooden cross, dripping blood from a thorn crown, and from his pierced side and impaled hands and feet. A Middle Eastern Judean, yet looking as Caucasian as this congregation. The taut muscles of his bare chest and long arms and legs reminded her of a champion swimmer. His sad eyes gazed upward.

"The body of Christ."

Her mother was in the crowd somewhere, no doubt watching with a full heart as her only child walked the path to salvation. Anita Nils, in her church clothes, wearing enough makeup to hide the bruises. The Jack bruises. Probably sitting next to one of her friends from Ladies Sodality, the only group he had let her join.

"The body of Christ."

At the head of the line now was Arminda Larch. Denise had never before seen her in a dress, Arminda being more a jeans-and-sneakers girl. Mixing it up with the boys on the ball field behind St. Alfonzo's, cursing and spitting, as loud and crude as any of them. She had a pug face, and a chunky frame. When Arminda turned from the priest with the wafer in her mouth, Denise fought the urge to gawk at her legs. They were whiter than Denise's dress.

According to the transubstantiation doctrine, the priest literally alters the substance of the wafer into the Son of God's flesh. At first, the idea of eating a man's body had frightened and repelled her. But seeing as how all these people accepted it, she gradually came to accept it herself. Now she looked forward to it with a thrill in her belly, like the first time she had lined up with Mom at a Ferris wheel.

The altar boy looked slightly bored. Ted something-or-other. She knew him by sight. She remembered he had a faint scar on one cheek, and she had romanticized it as a dueling scar. But he was a fifth-grader, and fifth-graders were practically adults from her perspective. Another race altogether.

As she knelt on the pliant hassock, Ted held a brass paten under her chin.

"The body of Christ," Father Lipman said, holding up the host, his piercing blue eyes the only bright specks of color in his pallid face.

"Amen," she said, opening her mouth.

In placing the wafer, an edge of one of Father Lipman's fingers briefly touched her tongue.

She rose and returned to her pew and knelt again, her mind racing. The host dissolved against the roof of her mouth. Not at all how she had imagined it. But now she was one of them, cleansed and pure. One of the faithful, bathed in the glow of the holy Eucharist. One of the initiated.

One of the man-eaters.

***

"Eddie, would you mind helping a customer?"

He wished Taylin Lumen, his supervisor, would call him Edmund. EDMUND was clearly typed on his *May I Help You?* badge. It was her ham-handed attempt to be personable with him. Three years of familiarity at Harbo's Garden Center gave her a degree of entitlement, he supposed, though when other workers tried calling him by that nickname, he would cast them the evil eye Grandam had taught him. Doing so never failed to stop the behavior cold in its tracks.

"Of course." He turned from the rose of Sharon hibiscus bush he was attending. Some idiot on the morning shift had over-watered it and placed where it received little sunshine. Luckily, he had caught the mistakes in time, poured off the excess water and relocated it to a sunny location.

"What type of fertilizer should I buy for these?" The customer had two potted tiger lilies in her shopping cart and she gestured to them in a flitting, birdlike manner.

She was a white woman, about Grandam's age but blessed with better health. Stout and gray-haired, she wore a pink pants suit and a hat that, save for the presence of a silk rose, might be mistaken for a bellboy's cap.

"Are you planting them outside?" Edmund reached over and rotated one of the pots, so the leaves wouldn't rub against the edge of the cart. "Yes."

"Then you shouldn't need fertilizer unless your soil is very poor. Tiger lilies are hardy. They grow in the wild. Keep the soil moist and keep an eye out for slugs and beetles."

"Is there anything else I need to know?"

"Do you have a cat?"

"Yes. Mr. Frizzy."

"You'll want to keep Mr. Frizzy from the plants. Tiger lilies are poisonous to cats."

"Mr. Frizzy is an indoor cat."

"Then you should have no problems."

She eyed Edmund as if sizing him up, her hands on her hips. "You seem to know a lot about these plants. What else can you tell me?"

"Some people believe smelling tiger lilies can give you freckles."

She laughed. A pleasant, chimey laugh that broke her serious mien. "Well, then, I'll take care to enjoy them from a distance." She squinted at this badge. "Thank you, Edmund. You've been most helpful."

He nodded to her and returned to the hibiscus bush.

"Eddie."

Damn. Taylin again.

She looked barrel-bodied in her orange supervisor's vest. Her hair, somewhere between brown and black, was wiry and badly in need of professional attention. "There are some ficuses on the dock that don't look right to me," she said. "Give them a look, will you?"

He carefully wiped his hands with a cloth. "Of course," he said. Sometimes he was thankful that Saturdays were his half-days.

He returned the cloth to the pocket of his apron.

That evening he brought home groceries from Mort's. A bean-soup mix, almond milk, a loaf of pumpernickel, strawberry jam. When he entered the apartment, Grandam was watching Judge Judy on the television. The illumination from the television screen, strobe-like in its effect, lit her in her rocking chair. She was sans comforter now, no doubt having returned it to her bed, and instead wore a shawl over her

13

shoulders. He kissed her on her forehead. The heavy curtains were drawn, and rather than open them, he turned on the Tiffany lamp.

He feigned interest as Judge Judy read the riot act to an Asian man who had damaged his roommate's car and owed back rent.

"I'll fix supper, Grandam," he said after a minute. "I bought some of that bean soup you like."

When dinner was ready, he took her soup over to her rocking chair and set it on a TV tray, then he fetched himself a steamy bowlful and sat on the loveseat. She turned off the television and they ate in silence for a while.

"Tell me about the raids, Grandam," he said, lifting a spoon of broth to his lips.

She'd learned these stories of the old ways from her mother and her own grandam. Yet there was a vitality to her narrations that seemed drawn from some genetic memory.

She sipped from her spoon, chewed a bean thoughtfully, swallowed. "Our people called themselves the Kai-Tangata, which means 'hunters of men.' We practiced long hours with the spear and the bow and the cudgel, and anyone of us was a match for any outlier who dared challenge us. As in all things, we were of one mind and acted as one organism, like the pulsing jellyfish, each of us a stinging tentacle ready to strike."

She scraped the bottom of her soup bowl and thought for a moment.

"There was another tribe, on another part of the island. The Koroghori. These were our sworn enemies. Though the Koroghori, by and large, kept to their part of the island and the Kai-Tangata kept to our part of the island, human nature, of course, invites disputes. Territorial and what have you. Tempers flared. There were confrontations; threats and rock-throwing, and sometimes full-blown skirmishes. Occasionally we raided their village, burning huts and capturing Koroghori prisoners. And when we did, the Koroghori knew they would never see these people again."

She raised the bowl to her lips and drained off the last of the broth.

14

"We would take them back to the village and lock them in the gated ossuary, the cave where we kept all our bones, and we forced them to sit in the shadow of death while we made our preparations."

She held out her soup bowl to him.

"Would you like some more, Grandam?"

"Perhaps a half-bowl, if you wouldn't mind. It's delicious, Edmund."

He went to the kitchenette and ladled a generous half-portion for her. When he returned, he could see she was beginning to lose her train of thought.

"You locked the Koroghori prisoners in the bone cave," he prodded gently.

"Yes. We made them wait in the ossuary among the great piles of bones. Through the gate, they could see us, talking up the coming feast excitedly. They could see the special fire we were preparing, the spit and the cooking tools. When dark came, we painted our faces like red skulls and donned necklaces and anklets of human teeth. We danced past the cave, taunting them, as the flames of the fire licked upward in the night."

She squinted into her soup as if her bowl were a portal into the past.

"We rattled the gate and made menacing faces at them. Sometimes one of them fainted or vomited, or their bladder gave out. By the time the gate opened, these brave Koroghori warriors could often be led away like sheep, their legs rubbery, tears streaming from their bulging eyes." Grandam smiled. "Before we consumed them, we first consumed their dignity."

A fierceness came to her old gray eyes.

"If the warrior was male, we spread him on the ground and took a dagger to his genitals. We sliced these off and held them up for him to see, held them for the other prisoners to see as well. Then we gave them to the children to play with. They would run around, tossing them to each other and giggling, getting blood from the wrinkled thing on their bellies and faces."

She was quiet for a while, and he could see he was losing her.

15

"Edmund, I'm tired. Would you mind if I watched TV for a while?"

"Not at all," he said, though in truth he wanted to hear more about the torture and the feast. But her eyes were red, and her eyelids were getting crusty. "I need to go on the computer anyway, Grandam."

He scrolled the news sites, read his email. She finished her soup, and set the tray down on the threadbare carpet beside her. Partway through a commercial for adult diapers, she began to doze. Soon she was sound asleep, snoring softly.

He plugged in the USB drive.

Off and on, all day long, he had been composing his message to MsBathory, agonizing over every word. He went to the Forlorn Flesh Fetishist, looked up her post, and began to type.

Chapter Two

T he madman awoke on the side of the road, the sound of hoofbeats still echoing in his head.

He was lying in a ditch where passing cars couldn't see him, which was good, and there was no blood on him anywhere, which was also good.

He knew he was a half-mile from Barrytown, Illinois, because a reflective road sign nearby proudly proclaimed: BARRYTOWN 1/2 MI.

He considered hitching but decided instead that walking would help him clear his head.

It was a cool late-spring morning, and aside from a grass stain on one knee, he was in remarkably fine condition. As he walked, the heels of his cowboy boots kicked up loose gravel. He ran a hand through his dusty-blond hair and tried to remember what had happened last night.

He recalled being in a bar in an Indiana border town. A country-western bar called the Saddle Spur. He was drinking tap beer and watching rows of half-in-the-bag Hoosiers line dance to Randy Travis' "Cowboy Boogie." It was a catchy tune, and he might have been humming along with it when a swarthy-faced scarecrow of a fellow about his age pulled up at the next stool and tipped his black Stetson. "Howdy," he said.

The madman smiled. The Indiana cowboy took this as a welcoming sign.

"My name's Bill Griggs, but my friends call me Buster."

He shook hands with Bill Griggs and gave him one of the names he went by; he wasn't sure which one. Sometimes, he wasn't even sure himself what his real name was. But he knew it today: Milo Castellanos. He could even spell it.

Buster Griggs—*okay, maybe a tad older than him, maybe in his early thirties?*—looked back at him in the semi-dark with subdued, dove-gray eyes. His cheeks were pockmarked, and he had a three-day growth of beard that lent him a rugged look.

He saw at once that Buster was a lonesome soul, just like him.

"You from around here?" Buster asked.

They talked, watched the line dancers perform another song, had a few beers together. Swapped lies. He felt drawn to the rangy young fellow. He hated giving in to this kind of hunger because it sometimes led to the other kind. The kind that made him unique.

Baba Yaga.

But he did give in. He remembered when they left the Saddle Spur together, remembered the jukebox playing "Why Don't We Get Drunk and Screw?"

The next thing he recalled was their bodies pressing together behind a silver Ford F-150 in the shadow cast by the parking-lot lights. Smelling Buster's cologne, the spicy lavender of Paul Sebastian. His tongue flicked light sweat from Buster's neck.

And that's all he remembered of the encounter. But a dull hollowness in his groin filled in one of the missing pieces.

Milo followed beside the asphalt approach road to a bridge. Now he was on Main Street. To the left was a forest of white oak and birch, to the right a strip of businesses far as the eye could see. He checked the pockets of his jeans and found a money clip, thick with tens and twenties, and a stack of rubber-banded charge cards and drivers' licenses, including one in the name of Ben Dribbin. He also found a Deadwood, South Dakota, keyring containing three brass keys. Ben Dribbin's house keys.

He considered tossing the keys into the woods but returned them to his pocket.

He walked toward Barrytown proper, toward the crawling traffic and the clusters of signs and businesses. It always felt fresh, walking into a new town. Now he was on sidewalk, smiling and nodding to fellow pedestrians. He passed a gas station, a diner, a used car lot, the entry to a strip mall. Ahead was a hotel—the Snuggle Inn. Cute name.

At the counter of the Snuggle Inn, he rang the bell for service.

Out stepped a young woman, twentyish. Her shoulder-length hair, dyed purple, was pulled back in a ponytail. Pert nose with a ring through one nostril, brilliant smile, large eyes, scrubbed pink skin. Her *May I Help You?* badge read: PAMELA.

He smiled back at her, familiar urges bubbling up within him.

He wondered what she tasted like.

> Chapter Three

E dmund finished repotting a heartleaf philodendron and was brushing clean his hands when the grating voice erupted behind him. "Eddie?"

Taylin, the bane of his Harbo's workday, tilted her head to one side. "Pretty busy today, isn't it?"

He looked around at the store full of people, as if just noticing them. He nodded. "Pretty busy. What's up?"

"Do I have to have a reason to talk with you?" she asked. "After all this time, aren't we friends?"

Well, friends *might be pushing it, but why make her feel bad?* "Of course, it's just that, as you say, we're pretty busy right now."

She grinned at him, baring a chipped side tooth. "Well, Mr. Serious, do you remember that old woman from the other day? The one in the pink pants suit?"

He thought for a moment. "Yes. She was asking about tiger lilies."

"Well, she's back, and she's asking for you."

He frowned. "Alright."

He followed Taylin to the customer service desk, where the woman waited, this time in an egg-yolk yellow pants suit and a matching hat with a spray of silken tickseed daisies. Her face lit up when she saw him. "Edmund, there you are."

"You can call him Eddie, if you like," Taylin said, "you being a good customer and all."

He felt his face flush. She *had* to know he hated that name.

"But his badge says Edmund."

Taylin grinned again, rolling her eyes when the customer wasn't looking.

"Gotta run," she said, and headed off toward the grass-seed aisle. Wearing a puzzled expression, the woman in the pants suit watched her leave.

Birdlike. That was the only word he could think of that captured the old woman's way of moving. By fits and starts.

"How's Mr. Frizzy?" Edmund asked.

Her face lit up again. "Oh, Mr. Frizzy is quite well. I've followed your instructions and made sure he gets nowhere near the tiger lilies. Though to be honest, it's just *tiger lily* now. I'm afraid I may have killed one of them. By accident, of course. I wouldn't want you to think I'm one of these people who go around killing plants for the fun of it. Certainly not."

"I would never think that." He'd never even heard of such a thing before.

"Well, you see, I'm not any good at gardening. When I was a girl, we had a lovely garden. My mother was an excellent gardener. Her rose bushes once won a ribbon at the state fair. But I never picked up the knack. I sometimes think plants shiver when I approach them."

He expected her to smile, but she didn't.

"How can I help you? Did you want another tiger lily?"

"No. I mean, maybe. Not just yet. I was wondering if you'd be willing to look at our gardens and give your professional assessment. Any suggestions would be most helpful."

"Go to your house?"

"Yes. We'd pay you, of course. Elon—that's my husband, Elon Bennett—thinks we should get a professional opinion before proceeding any further in developing them."

"Well, I'm no landscaper, but I might be willing to have a look. Maybe this weekend? During the week I work till six most nights, then I usually make dinner for my grandam, but I only work a half-day on Saturday, and Sundays I'm free. I could maybe swing by on Saturday afternoon. Where do you live?"

She had come prepared. She handed Edmund a cream-colored card with an address and a phone number on it. "We live in Minnetonka. Just off the lake. If you like, we could send a car for you."

"A car?"

"Yes. We have a driver. His name is Rudy. He's waiting for me in the parking lot now if you'd like to meet him."

Edmund pocketed the card. "I have some spider plants that need feeding just now, Mrs. Bennett. But I'd be happy to look at your garden on Saturday afternoon."

"Saturday it is."

***

Sometime after her First Communion, Denise went to Trevor Bates' birthday party. She was surprised he had invited her, but later she found out Trevor's mom had made him invite all the neighborhood kids. Denise's gift to him was a model airplane. When he opened the present, he seemed to like it. Well enough anyway to study the box.

Trevor was a third-grader, with a little sister whose name she couldn't remember. Patricia maybe. She was only in kindergarten, and though the girls didn't usually play together, they did the day of his party. They were in an upstairs bedroom, switching out Barbie outfits and accessories, pushing the plastic dolls around in a little Barbie car, and talking for the Barbies in adult voices, when Trevor's sister suddenly said, "Do you want to see a rat?"

Denise scrunched her nose at this. "A rat. You mean a sewer rat?" Denise had seen one of those before in the basement of an old house in which they had once lived. She was not eager to revisit that experience.

"No, silly—a pet. Trevor has a pet rat that just had babies. Tiny baby rats." Trevor's sister approximated their size with a finger and thumb. "Do you want to see?"

"Sure." But she was secretly uneasy.

Pamela Bates, that was her name! With the name, Denise's memory gained lucidity. She could picture Pamela clearly:

23

underweight, even for an adolescent girl; straw-colored hair; eyes almost big enough for a Margaret Keane painting.

They went down a hallway to Trevor's room. Baseball cards in transparent sleeves were pinned to a wall in neat rows. A toy chest overflowed with Matchbox cars, sports equipment, plastic army men, and Lego bricks. A shelf held a collection of G.I. Joes in a variety of uniforms, some holding guns, some holding canteens, some holding binoculars. At the foot of Trevor's bed was a chest of drawers that supported a modest glass terrarium filled with wood shavings, a metal rodent wheel, and a fluffy white rat.

"Come on," Trevor's sister said.

Denise stepped cautiously to the glass, still not keen on this viewing. But what she saw amazed her. The mother rat, rather than displaying maternal behavior such as grooming or nursing or crouching over her young charges to keep them safe and warm, was chewing on one of them. She tore away a bloody strip of the pup's tiny head with her long, buff-colored incisors as the baby rat continued to squirm. She crunched on the bones, sucked the gore, stuffed her struggling offspring, one gulp at a time, into her working jaws and down her throat. She swallowed thickly, viscera gleaming on her white fur.

Trevor's sister screamed. Adult chaperones and young partygoers thundered up the steps. They quickly filled the small bedroom and stood gasping around the glass tank, staring in horror as the mother rat worked a second progeny into her maw.

Turning from the glass, Denise smiled up at the gapers and said gleefully, "She's *eating* them!"

Chapter Four

Milo awoke to the sound of a voice speaking the name of a familiar town. The sky outside his hotel window was a darkling field of stars. Fast-food wrappers crinkled under him as he sat up in bed. He appeared to have shoveled three burgers, two orders of french fries, and a slice of apple pie into his gut. Must have dozed off sometime after his feast. His short-term memory was getting spotty again.

He was glad he'd remembered to eat. Sometimes, in the sway of one of his spells, he didn't eat for days. Nothing in the way of traditional foodstuffs, anyway.

He collected the wrappers, balled them together, and fired the resultant sphere across the room into a trash bin. Three points.

On the screen, emergency medical technicians were pushing a gurney from a forest. On the gurney was an orange body bag. He scratched his blond head and focused on the television reporter.

"The victim was 37-year-old Benjamin Dribbin of Maitland, South Dakota, a father of three, who was last seen in Indianapolis, where he attended a realtor's convention. He is believed to have left the Indianapolis Convention Center sometime on June 21st or 22nd, in the company of a person or persons unknown. The body was discovered in a wooded area near White Lick Creek in Plainfield, Indiana. According to police, the corpse was dismembered and, apparently, partially consumed, making officials suspect that this was the work of the so-called Midwest Butcher. However, this has yet to be confirmed."

Milo found a cold fry on the bedspread and ate it.

Then he pulled out the dead man's driver's license and examined the photo. Ben Dribbin, realtor, an odd-looking little fellow, hair thinning, eyes watery. And that mustache! Like something you'd see in an old movie. William Powell in *The Thin Man.*

Would you buy a used duplex from this man? Milo grinned.

He took out the keys and examined the ring. A souvenir of Deadwood, it was shaped like a sheriff's badge, riddled with holes meant to be bullet holes. He wondered whether old Ben even owned a gun. He supposed most people from South Dakota did. Too bad for Ben that he wasn't packing that night. It might have saved him. Come to think of it, probably not.

Before his nap, the day had passed at breakneck speed. He did some light shopping, bought himself a denim jacket, a pack of disposable vinyl gloves, and a change of socks and underwear. Next, he loaded up on snacks at the local Walgreens before heading to the liquor store. The burger joint was his last stop.

When he returned to the Snuggle Inn, Pamela—the girl with the nose ring and the purple hair—was gone. Her replacement was a somewhat haggard-looking, middle-aged redhead in oversized glasses and a faded blouse. She was standing at the counter, reading a book when he came in. *The Seven Habits of Highly Effective People.*

Good for her, looking to improve herself. Though perhaps that boat has already sailed.

She looked up at him and smiled with her eyes. Seeing he needed no help, she went back to her book. He noticed a faint pulse in her neck. It nearly took the breath from him.

He remembered thinking wryly, *Decisions, decisions.*

He also remembered thinking, *I wonder where Pamela is?*

He got up from the bed and turned off the television. He looked out the hotel window into the parking lot below. A teen couple wearing the smocks of a local hardware store crossed between cars on newly laid asphalt. The girl feigned disinterest as the boy flitted around her, talking excitedly with exaggerated gestures. Milo couldn't hear what they were saying, but he surmised their shifts at the hardware store must have just ended, and the boy was trying to talk her into something. A date maybe. A popcorn movie. *The Black Panther* or *The Avengers*. He tried to read her, but he had no idea whether she would give in to the pleading. She'd mastered the no-tell face of her gender. However, to Milo, she looked well out of the boy's league.

He wondered what it would be like to take two of them at once. *Baba Yaga would be so pleased.*

Such a bold move would require careful planning and ideal conditions.

He decided to shelve the idea.

For now.

Entering the parking lot was his purple-haired miss, Pamela, in a faux-suede moto jacket, rugged but feminine. Nice choice. She was talking on her phone, car keys in her hand, approaching a Nissan hatchback, maybe 2007 or 2008. A tried-and-true vehicle, utilitarian, easy to park. A cheerful blue with little or no rust on the wheel wells, recently run through a car wash. That was the key, proper maintenance. He bet she had the oil changed every 3,000 miles. She was the second owner, he guessed, and the first had rarely driven it. It really was in excellent shape for a vehicle over ten years old.

Pamela put her key in the door lock and twisted. Before she entered the Nissan, she glanced up and spotted Milo in the window. She flashed her brilliant smile and waved. Then the car door opened, and she slid in, smooth as a breeze.

As she pulled out of the parking lot, Milo noticed the backseat passenger-side window was half-open.

The radio alarm clock in his room told him it was 10:13 p.m.

His mind started ticking.

Chapter Five

W hen she read "Hansel and Gretel" in the third grade, Denise felt a shift inside her, as if something in her belly became unanchored and free-floating.

Of course, she had heard the story before, the sanitized, cartoon version.

But the old book in the Hennepin County library poked holes in the tale and suggested a startlingly different story.

Jack was out of the picture by this time, though Carlos wasn't much of an improvement. He slept most of the day, appearing in the late afternoon, rumpled, in paint-stained jeans and one of his flannel shirts, his calloused toes huge and hairy, with horny nails. He grinned a little too broadly at her, and when his gaze fell on her, she could feel his twinkling eyes crawling over her skin.

The library was one of her favorite places: sunny, quiet, all the books a young girl could ever want, and everybody left her alone. She especially liked that last part. She didn't have to be on her best behavior; didn't have to play the good daughter, the good pupil, the good friend. She didn't have to pay attention to things that didn't interest her. She could hunker in a corner with a stack of books— unencumbered of all fakery and deception—and read to her heart's content. As a bonus, it was a place where she could learn about things adults didn't want her to know.

That day, for instance, when Denise's mother had dropped her off at the library for the afternoon, she'd learned that a dark world hid beneath the veneer of an innocuous fairy tale.

The library book made plain what an ugly mess "Hansel and Gretel" really was.

First off, the kids didn't get lost; they were abandoned in the woods by their parents. Famine had swept the countryside, and their mom and dad decided they could no longer afford to feed the kiddies, so they abandoned them to starve to death and probably be eaten by wild animals.

Some versions of the tale have the mother plotting to eat the children, with the father whisking Hansel and Gretel deep into the woods to spare them this fate and give them at least the slimmest chance at survival. He lit a fire for them, went off to gather more wood, and never came back. *Gee, thanks, Dad.*

Denise imagined what it must have been like, hungry and shivering by a fire as blackest night descended. Wolves howling, owls hooting, feral scrabbling noises in the shadows all around.

In the woods, Hansel, the alleged voice of reason, calms Gretel, who, in typical fairy-tale fashion, is a maiden who tearfully falls apart in times of stress.

Hansel tells her that everything will be alright because, unbeknownst to their father, he has left a trail of pebbles that they can follow back home. Hansel filled his pockets with the stones after overhearing his parents plot their demise the night before.

Why would the children want to return to parents who already tried to kill them once?

When they return, their father again leads them into the woods—this time deeper—and again abandons them. Hansel, assuming this would happen again, has left a trail, not of pebbles this time, but of bread crumbs to follow back home—*These kids really couldn't take a hint, could they?*—only birds eat the bread crumbs, so Hansel's scheme goes for naught.

The siblings wander in the woods in search of sustenance. Perhaps they find some berries or nuts, but not enough to slake their hunger. They come at last to a house made of gingerbread or, in early versions, cake. Either way, a sugary treat, and immediately they begin gobbling up the house.

Meanwhile, living in the house is a witch. She comes out, posing as a kind old woman, and welcomes them inside for a proper meal.

After Hansel and Gretel eat their fill of pancakes, the witch—who reveals herself as not such a kind woman after all—holds them captive, forcing them to sweep and do other chores while she fattens them up for a future dinner.

Why they don't just eat their way out of the house when the witch isn't looking remains a mystery.

One day, the witch puts a big old cauldron of water on the stove. She eyes Hansel, who she's now keeping in a chicken coop. From the hungry look on the witch's face, Gretel can see where this is heading. The witch tells Gretel to crawl inside the oven to make sure it's hot enough to bake bread. Gretel pretends she doesn't understand the command. Finally, in frustration, the witch hops into the hot oven to demonstrate. Gretel closes the oven door and, the next thing you know, the witch is burned to a cinder.

Hansel and Gretel escape the witch's lair with a sack full of gold and jewels, somehow find their way back home—in some versions with the aid of a magical swan—and are greeted by their "loving" parents. Now that they're rich, the folks can once again afford to have kids. *Yay!* You have to think, though, that Hansel and Gretel must have spent the rest of their adolescent nights sleeping with one eye open.

Later versions morphed the mother into a stepmother (apparently the Grimm brothers came to feel that motherhood should be sacred, and changed all their evil mothers to stepmothers), and they put the lion's share of the blame for the attempted infanticide on her. However, the dad is obviously complicit in the scheme. Some versions have the stepmom dying during the kids' absence, and the father becoming repentant for his part in the deeds.

However the brothers Grimm chose to close the door on this troubling adventure, what Denise found especially interesting was the basis for the story.

While bits and pieces were swiped from French and Swedish folklore, the story's main vein seemed to come from a Russian yarn called "Vasilisa the Beautiful," in which an evil stepmother sends her stepdaughter into the woods on an errand, directing her to a house that belongs to Baba Yaga, a notorious cannibal witch.

It turns out that Baba Yaga is not just a witch, but a mystical fusing of assorted pagan deities and black magic. A pre-Christian demigod who holds God and the Devil in equal contempt. She lives in a house that rotates on chicken legs, she roams the night skies in a mortar, wielding a pestle as both a rudder and a cudgel.

Her appearance is hideous, with a long, swollen nose, iron teeth sharp as razors, one leg of bare bone, and withered pendulous breasts. And, of course, Baba Yaga thrives on the blood and flesh of children and young women, and she kills without mercy or remorse, often on a whim.

The fence around her house is made from the bones of her victims and topped with skulls, except for one bone post, which waited to be crowned with the skull of Baba Yaga's next victim.

How cool was that?

***

The hotel stationery would have to do. The paper was white with the hotel's name in cursive type at the top. (Milo had read that schoolchildren weren't taught cursive nowadays; to them this stationery might as well be written in hieroglyphics.) It was only a 20-pound bond, white with the hotel's name in cursive type at the top. He preferred something stouter than this, which was a little too see-through for his liking. Some hotels offered luxurious, textured stationery with embossed lettering. A hotel he'd once stayed at in Yellow Springs, Ohio, provided pastel lavender letterhead with not only the hotel's name in raised ink but also a flourish of hummingbirds in one corner. It was a thing of beauty.

He pulled on the snug, vinyl gloves, lifted several sheets of stationery from the bedside drawer, and carried them to the meager desk. He folded each just below the hotel address, then carefully tore along the folds. He discarded the pieces with the address. Now he had five sheets of plain white paper. Untraceable. He turned them so the ragged tears were at the bottom.

Then he poured himself a healthy slug of Evan Williams bourbon and began composing in his head.

Day Two at the Snuggle Inn was uneventful but not altogether tedious.

The old urges were churning freely in him now, distracting him from his hunger, but he'd forced himself to eat something. At the hotel's breakfast bar, he helped himself to a cup of bland coffee and four slices of toast topped with gelatinous cubes of strawberry jelly. These he carried back on a tray to his room for private consumption: the fewer people with an opportunity to eyeball him, the better. Along the way, he snatched a Sun-Times and a Tribune from the hotel lobby.

Pamela was busy behind the counter, soothing an agitated hotel maid who had found something untoward that a guest had deposited in one of the room's coffeemakers. *People can be so rude.*

The newspapers featured extensive, front-page stories on the fate poor Ben Dribbin had suffered at the Midwest Butcher's hands. There were sidebars on Ben's life, photos of his wife and children, touching eulogies from friends and neighbors. All designed to pull at the heartstrings, while alternately thrilling and chilling the reader with grisly details of the crime.

The coverage in the newspapers, as always, was much more thorough than what television news offered up. The papers spared no detail of the slaughter, provided relevant background information, speculated on where police thought the Butcher was now, and where he might strike next. As usual, this guesswork was mistaken, their best hunch having him still somewhere in Indiana.

He needed to move soon to stay a step ahead of them.

One of the papers ran a reasonably extensive sidebar on the Butcher's previous slayings, a recap of the past 12 years. Twenty brief profiles with mug shots. Of course, there was no mention of the uncredited wet work he had done. That was by his design. Better not to show the public all his cards. He wouldn't want his one life to bleed over into the other.

Of course, there was no mention of Baba Yaga, who gifted him his calling.

The FBI was characteristically tight-lipped and stoic about the Dribbin murder. A spokeswoman for the bureau said only that they were pursuing leads and welcomed contact from anyone who might have information on the killing.

The policeman who discovered the body (or what remained of it) was so shaken he was undergoing trauma counseling. Milo grinned.

He picked up a pen that featured an advertisement for a Barrytown pizza parlor and began to write.

When he finished, he looked over his work:

Dear Mrs. Dribbin,

I thought you might be interested in further details regarding the death of your husband, Benjamin H. Dribbin. To allay your curiosity, I got your address from Ben's driver's license, which I am looking at right now. I must say the photo is not bad by license bureau standards.

I met Ben at an Indianapolis bar, the name of which I mustn't divulge due to personal security concerns. I'm sure you understand. When I met him, Ben was in excellent spirits. I found him talkative and personable in that smarmy, used-car-salesmen way he had. It was late, and he'd already been drinking for a few hours and was more than a little inebriated.

When I learned of his calling, I must confess that I gave him the impression I was interested in purchasing substantial real estate in South Dakota. He told me he knew the perfect territory for me, not far from Deadwood. I acted as if this keenly interested me, though, of course, I could not imagine living in such a godforsaken place as South Dakota.

I told him I was staying at a friend's house, and if he didn't mind giving me a lift there, we could use the ride to discuss details of the land deal he had in mind. He was too drunk to drive, and you really must caution your children about getting into cars with strangers. Bad idea, in my experience.

Of course, there was no friend. There was, however, an abandoned cabin on Wasatch Lake. I won't tell you how I knew the cabin would be there empty. Let's just say I did.

I recall Ben stopping in the darkened drive, asking me if I was sure this was the place. In reply, I reached out, put my hands around his skinny neck, and squeezed like the dickens. I didn't kill him there (what fun would that be?) but merely choked him until he was unconscious.

I dragged him into the cabin, removed his clothes, and tied him securely with three-strand polyester boat rope. Very strong. It was unseasonably cool that night, so I turned on the heat, enough to get the chill and dampness out of the air, then took off my own clothes and put them in a plastic garbage bag. You see, I didn't want to get them stained.

I found some coffee in a cabinet, made a pot, and sat at the table to wait for Ben to wake up.

I know what you're thinking: why didn't I just rouse him? Because that would diminish the pure shock value of him coming to his senses on his own and realizing that he is utterly helpless in the custody of a naked stranger. I always find this dawning on their faces to be priceless.

When he did wake up, I was not disappointed. His stupid face registered several degrees of fear and anguish as he put together the hopeless layers of his predicament. I stood over him and laughed, my manhood dangling over his prone torso. I sat on his stomach, and he looked up at me in horror.

I'll spare you some of the details here for the sake of my own privacy. Let's just say we became intimately acquainted with each other's taste and feel. I pity you, Mrs. Dribbin, for having to satiate yourself with that shriveled little thing of his. But I digress.

Once I'd taken him sexually, I turned him over and took a wire whisk to his buttocks (which I found to be surprisingly firm for a man of his age and condition). I whacked his butt with that whisk until there were scarlet stripes that blossomed with his blood. He was crying like a baby.

I could see this was starting to get messy, so I pulled down the plastic shower curtain from the bathroom and dragged him on top of it. He gibbered like an idiot, sputtering and prattling, begging me not to kill him.

I turned him over, sat on him again, and, with a carving knife, cut off his ears and nose and widened the slit of his mouth from ear to ear. He was bucking frantically, screaming, I recall, which mildly aroused me. Then he went unconscious again.

I stabbed him in the neck and sucked blood from him, drinking my fill. He moaned as I gouged out his eyes with a soup spoon. I rolled him over again and sliced off his buttocks—the portions of the bodies that I always especially enjoy eating. I cut off great slabs of meat from his thighs and calves, cut open his belly, and fished around in his slimy guts for his liver and kidneys. Then I reached up under his ribs for his heart and ripped it out. I wish I could say it was still beating, but it was not. Needless to say, sometime during all this carving and so on, poor Benjamin had given up his ghost.

I cut a little more meat from his arms and ribs and had a reasonably healthy stack of slabs and parts. I wrapped these in some old newspapers. I thought about partaking of some of the meat that night, but without onions and other vegetables, and the proper presentation, it would be a waste of precious flesh. Besides, I still needed to take a shower and clean up the cabin.

I chopped him up as best I could without a hacksaw and loaded him in the trunk in trash bags. The shower curtain had caught most of the blood, but not all. Luckily I found ample cleaning products under the sink. When I finished, the only sign of entry to the cabin was the missing shower curtain, which was too torn and bloody to save. That said, the place was cleaner when I left than when I arrived.

I'd already scouted the dumpsite in Plainfield. I had a pleasant hour or so driving there with the window open and the crisp night air in my teeth, but I had to hurry because dawn was already starting to break. After hauling the bags into the woods near White Lick Creek (what do you suppose that name signifies?), I drove the car someplace it wouldn't immediately attract suspicion. I won't say where but rest assured it was someplace clever.

One more thing: be sure to leave a light on for me. I may drop by the next time I'm in South Dakota.

Say hi to the kids for me.

Your friend,

The Butcher

***

"You must be the famous Mr. Frizzy." The calico cat rubbed against Edmund's leg, purring contentedly.

"He likes you," Elon Bennett observed cheerfully.

"I've always had a way with animals."

"Nonsense," Mr. Bennett said. "Mr. Frizzy is a *shrewd judge of character.*"

Edmund smiled and shrugged.

Animals had always been drawn to him and his casual Caribbean demeanor. Perhaps it was a scent he gave off. Once, at a coworker's house, someone had brought along an English mastiff bitch, an enormous dog, heavier than a Saint Bernard. The dog had no sooner entered the house when she waddled straight over to where Edmund sat and stood there with sad, rheumy eyes, expecting to be petted. The dog's head was monstrous, her tongue lolling like a flap of rubber. Edmund remembered thinking, as he reached out to lightly stroke the mastiff's head, that the animal could wolf down his fingers in a single snap.

The Bennetts' home displayed, as he expected, splendid taste. The furnishings were colonial antique, coffee-colored wood grains with delicate carvings along the edges. The tables were fitted with beveled glass, and decorated with vases and small trays of translucent, molded glassware. Torchiere and squat table lamps with matching shades trimmed in gold. A huge bay window looked down across a roadway onto Lake Minnetonka, the body of water made famous by Prince in the movie *Purple Rain.*

The overall appearance of the house was stately but not ostentatious.

"Adele tells me you're quite the expert on gardening," Mr. Bennett said. "Never had much luck with it myself. It requires a great deal of patience, and I've never had much of that. But I do enjoy flowers. Their splendid colors always bring a touch of warmth, especially on overcast days. Little dabs of color that bring joy to the heart, don't you agree, Edmund?"

Elon Bennett was living proof that over time mates come to resemble each other. Though hatless and bald on top, he was stout like his wife, about the same age, and moved with the same flitting, birdlike gestures. He wore a white shirt, open at the neck, tan trousers, and black wing-tipped Oxfords.

"The Buddha said, 'If we could see the miracle of a single flower clearly, our whole life would change.'"

"That's beautiful, Edmund. Are you a Buddhist?"

"No. Just a fan."

"Well, those Eastern fellows can teach us a lot."

Mrs. Bennett entered with three cups of tea balanced on a tray.

"Edmund and I were just discussing flowers, dear," Mr. Bennett said.

"Well, I hope you mentioned asters because a garden wouldn't be a garden without asters."

"Where's Rudy?" Mr. Bennett asked.

"I sent him into town with a grocery list. Why, did you need him for something?"

"If I had known you were sending him on errands, I would have put in an order for a few tins of sardines."

"They give you gas, Elon."

Mr. Bennett sulked. "Well, we'll need Rudy to give Edmund a ride home when we've finished inspecting the gardens."

"Don't pout. It's a short list. He'll be back in time. And I put down your horrid sardines."

Mr. Bennett's face brightened again. "That's very thoughtful of you, Adele."

After tea and light conversation, they inspected the gardens. There was one in the front and one in the back. Mrs. Bennett's lone tiger lily rose from the soil in the center of the front yard, like a drooping monolith, surrounded by smatterings of hardy perennials: red-purple asters; some Golden Light azaleas; spiky, globe-shaped Gardenview Scarlets; plump, pink peonies; and corn-colored black-eyed Susans. It was overgrown with all the usual garden banes: white clover, dandelions, Creeping Charlie, spurge. All in a mixture of their own making.

Edmund got down on one knee and inspected a clod of soil. It was lightly packed and still appeared to be rich in nutrients. Not like some of the urban soil he'd seen. He crumbled the clod in his hand. Not stony.

"Your soil is good, but I'd still suggest putting in some moisture-retentive potting mix to give new blooms a boost. Being on an incline, you should have adequate drainage. I see a hose near the front door, which should make watering easy. Looks like you have plenty of sunlight here. The lawn will need to be cultivated. You'll be digging, so make sure there are no power, water, or gas lines here. As far as types of flowers go, the perennials you have are fine, but they'll need to be transplanted. For the overall appeal, you'll want to stay within a three- or four-color range. Too many colors can make a garden look noisy. Plus some foliage plants to highlight the flowers. Ferns, elephant ears, maybe some ornamental grasses."

The next house over from the Bennetts' was quite a ways away. It was not as luxurious as the Bennett place, but still rich for Edmund's blood. An immense white colonial with gabled roofs, had it been a newer construction, it might qualify as a McMansion. In one upper window, the neighbor stood in silhouette, watching them.

"Who's that?" Edmund asked, indicating the figure with his chin.

"Oh, that's Yegor Dzhurmongaliev," Mr. Bennett said. "We call him George. Interesting character. Has a glass eye. He translates old Russian books into English. Been here nearly as long as we have, and we've been here since 1974. His people came over from the old country. He has something of a garden. Maybe you could offer him some advice, as well."

Mr. Bennett waved to George, and George waved back.

"If you ever meet him, Edmund," Mrs. Bennett said, "don't mention politics or religion. Once you get that man going on one of those subjects, there's no stopping him."

"You ready to look in the backyard?" Mr. Bennett asked.

They walked between the huge house and the three-car garage.

The backyard was maybe a half-acre, flat and shaded by broadleaf trees: bur oak and black walnut. A bit too many for Edmund's liking but some people just enjoyed trees. A patio extended from the back of the house, covered by a massive awning that let through stingy specks of sunlight. Quality outdoor furniture massed around a glass-topped table.

The Bennetts kept their garden tools in a small cottage with a bay window and stucco facing far back from the house.

They walked Edmund over to it, opened the door, and turned on the light.

Neatly arranged tools were hung on a wall and stacked in one corner: loppers and a pruning saw, pruning shears, a garden fork, hand trowels, gloves, shovels and spades, rakes, assorted hoes, an edger, a weeder, a garden knife, a leaf blower, garden scissors, extra hose, two wheelbarrows, a riding lawnmower, and a string trimmer. All top quality.

"Impressive," Edmund said.

The garden implements took up about a third of the space, and the remaining was living quarters. There was a bed, a table, two chairs, a small fridge and stove, and a sink. There was a bathroom in the back. It was all immaculately clean and cozy. "Does someone live out here?"

"Not now," Mrs. Bennett said. "Years ago, the former owner had a gardener who lived out here. We keep it up but no one's stayed out here since we've owned the place."

"It's well-insulated with a tile floor, and the bay window lets in a lot of natural light," Mr. Bennett added.

Edmund put his hands in his pockets and turned to the Bennetts. He eyed the pair for a minute. "What is it exactly you want me to do?"

"Adele and I were hoping we could talk you into putting in the gardens for us, and maintaining them as needed. You know, designing them, what have you. We would obviously pay you. You could even live here in the cottage, if you like."

"I have Grandam to take care of."

"Of course, you have other obligations," Mr. Bennett said, gesturing with open hands. "Whatever works for you. We'll be completely on your schedule. Adele and I would just be so happy to put things in the hands of a professional."

Mrs. Bennett blinked and smiled. "It would mean so much to us, Edmund, if you would agree to take this on."

What could he say? "Sure."

Chapter Six

Denise found it astounding that so many fairy tales revolved around the theme of cannibalism. *Who knew?*

During summer vacations, she spent days at the library.

If she arrived early, she could usually nab her favorite reading corner. On the rare occasions someone had already taken it, Denise felt out of sorts and would stare daggers the offender's way.

She usually brought a light lunch along (though eating in the library was technically forbidden) and consumed it on the sly, sometimes sitting for hours in her favorite spot, lost in her imaginary, literary la-la land.

Most fairy tales came from an oral tradition. The French writer Charles Perrault collected some of these in one of the first kiddie books. He wrote about an ogre who, in a drunken rampage, slit the throats of his seven daughters, mistakenly thinking they were seven boys he'd planned on eating the next day.

In one of its many versions, Little Red Riding Hood is tricked by the wolf (dressed as Grandma) into eating some of the real grandmother and drinking her blood. This part of the story was excised by Perrault, though he still ended his version with the wolf eating Red.

Just like that. The end.

At least it made more sense than a wandering woodsman discovering the wolf, chopping the creature open with his ax and liberating Red and Grandma *intact* from the wolf's belly.

In an early variant of "Sleeping Beauty," the prince's mother was a cannibal who ate her grandchildren. *Didn't see that one coming!*

In some of the more than 700 versions of "Cinderella" is a Tibetan Cindy-type story that has the heroine killing her mother by slicing off her breasts (some ogresses then consume the body). And, of course, "Hop o' My Thumb," an early telling of "Jack and the Beanstalk," features an ogre singing that old chestnut:

Fee, fau, fum
I smell the blood of an English man,
Be he alive or be he dead,
I'll grind his bones to make my bread.

From fairy tales, she moved on to Greek mythology. Titan Cronus, a.k.a. Saturn, ate his children and nephews, to keep them from challenging his throne. (Denise had tacked a haunting Goya image, *Saturn Eating His Son*, on her bedroom wall until Mom made her take it down.)

In some brotherly wrangling over adultery and power, Atreus cooked up a meal for Thyestes that featured Thyestes' kids as the main course. Tantalus served up his son for the gods to enjoy. In *The Odyssey*, Homer relates how a giant cyclops grabs one of Odysseus' men in each hand, smashes their skulls together, and devours them. The list goes on and on.

Then there was the greater field of cannibalism in other countries' mythologies.

The Romanian character Muma Pădurii made soup out of little girls. Australian Aborigines talked of a cannibal giant named Thardid Jimbo. Vedic myth featured the Rakshasas, cannibals and vampires who drank blood from human skulls. The Kwakwaka'wakw in British Columbia told the story of Dzunuḵwa, an ogress who collected kiddos in a basket to eat. Moari mythology included tales of a cannibal thunder goddess named Whaitiri. And, of course, there was always

Denise's favorite, the Russian witch-demon Baba Yaga, by far the most colorful of these cannibal beings.

Over time, Denise came to devour (*LOL!*) cannibalism in every flavor: folk tales; religious tracts; literature (even Shakespeare had his "Titus Andronicus" and Melville his *Typee*); historical exposés of the Aztecs, the Maoi of Easter Island, the sorcerers of Guyana, the bush tribes of the Congo Basin, the Waris of the Amazon, the headhunters of the Fiji Islands, the Cannibal Gardeners of ancient New Guinea, et al.

Urban legends; serial killers.

She read about the Donner party, the Andes airplane-crash survivors, Sweeny Todd, the digging up of graves in colonial Jamestown during the Starving Time, the eating of prisoners during wars (from Biblical days to World War II).

Some ate corpses out of respect, some out of hunger, others out of a desire to absorb traits from the dead.

The study of cannibalism in all its forms became a topic of endless fascination for Denise throughout her adolescence and into high school. Through all the Jacks and Carloses her mom dragged home, through catechism, braces, and a half-hearted stint as a Brownie (from which she was excommunicated for jumping up and down on her den mother's couch). Through roller skates, ten-speed bikes, a tonsillectomy, video games, sleepovers, and fumbling adventures with boys.

In her exploration of all things cannibal, she even found a few treatises in defense of cannibalism: "Why is it that animals, from spiders to lemurs to our cousins the apes, are allowed to eat of their own species, while *Homo sapiens* deny themselves this practice, instead squandering valuable nutrients to boxes in the earth?"

Why, indeed?

***

From CannibalJanet in Pickelscott, Shropshire, U.K.: "Greetings from your future tasty tidbit. Do you prefer your flesh spongy or callused, Raoul? Because I can offer a little of both. I'm wondering whether to apply lotion, but I'm afraid the chemicals might flavor the meat. Maybe I should use some tenderizer from the grocery store? I'm hoping that I can join you in at least part of your meal, like Meiwes and Brades. I rather fancy the idea of eating myself to death. Or would you prefer I play the long pig, and you play the chef?"

Still no reply from MsBathory.

Chapter Seven

S he came to Milo in fever dreams, transcending time and place, her knotted, gray braids uncoiling like Medusa's fanged serpents, her red eyes glowing like gateways to hell, her cracked and ancient visage glaring at him, her metal teeth gleaming. Sometimes her image was clear as day; sometimes, it was all distorted, watery, and warped as if viewed through carnival glass, through fog and prisms, as if reflected in misshapen mirrors. Snarling and clawing at him from her ragged depths.

She came to him now, and he knew what she wanted. What she always wanted.

So taken was he by this vision that when it diffused, for a moment Milo struggled to recall where he was. Was he still in Indiana? Was he with Buster Griggs at the Saddle Spur? Or with Ben Dribbin in the cabin? Or what was the name of that little boy in Ohio?

He let his eyes focus on the electric-yellow bench that faced him from the other side of the table. Beyond the bench was the back of a man's head, balding at the scalp's vertex, and across from the man sat a middle-aged woman in a light jacket, wearing a worried expression.

Her sharp eyes were on Milo.

How long had he been out this time?

"More coffee?" The waitress, a pleasant-eyed chubby girl with a shiny forehead, held out a pot.

"Why not?"

He leaned back and offered the worried-looking woman in the next booth a sheepish smile. She looked away.

He turned toward the waitress. Her *May I Help You?* badge read: LILLY. "I seem to be a little out of it today."

"Daydreaming is allowed," Lilly said with a grin. "All the best people do it."

He sipped the coffee, shuffling his thoughts. Barrytown, that was it, in Illinois. He'd left Buster down the road in Indiana, and Ben Dribbin was dead in Plainfield. He was staying at the Snuggle Inn, where a purple-haired girl named Pamela worked behind the counter. His equilibrium gradually returned.

It was late afternoon. He'd spent the morning outside of town, scouting secluded locations in the woods, which bore the fanciful name Fairview Garden Park. The area appeared largely ignored by groundskeepers and the general public.

He'd followed a labyrinth of trails until he'd discovered one that fed deep into the trees to a stony creek that ran with shallow water. What was it with him and creeks, all of a sudden? Something from his childhood, he guessed. Or maybe it was just coincidence, if one believed in such a thing.

Either way, it was tranquil, a spot for young children to chase butterflies or catch crawfish in plastic beer cups. He had sat with his boot heels in the streaming water and thought of sweet Pamela. *Baba Yaga wanted her.* So did he.

He was starting to get a headache. The restaurant was too brightly lit.

There was a small pool of blood on his plate from a half-eaten steak. He soaked the blood up with a roll, ate it, licked his fingers, had one last go at the coffee, and then rose, laying down a five for the waitress. The woman with the worried expression studied him as he got up.

He settled his bill at the front and stepped out into the partly sunny day.

From the hardware store, he bought a utility knife and duct tape. He requested his purchase be double-bagged. Next door at a department store, he added to his acquisitions a hammer, a double-

48

braided nylon rope, and a cheap canvas tote bag. And a handful of Zagnut candy bars, which he hadn't seen anywhere since he was a boy. These purchases were also double-bagged. He would need the plastic bags for later.

Then he mailed his letter.

As he walked through the Snuggle Inn's parking lot, he glanced at the blue Nissan. The rear passenger window was still half-open. *Yes!*

He carried his bags back to his room and unpacked them. He laid his purchases out on the bed and repacked everything in the canvas tote. Then he waited, peeling the wrapper from a Zagnut.

Pamela got off work at 10 o'clock, plenty of time to wipe down the hotel room and to dispose of any napkins or other traces that could be linked back to him. And plenty of time for a quick nap.

He was, after all, looking forward to a very taxing night.

Chapter Eight

R udy was a colorful guy, to say the least. He was older than the Bennetts, a veteran of World War II, but apparently not on the Allied side. When a cop raised one hand to stop traffic, Rudy raised his own hand and responded, "Heil."

Whatever his past affiliations, Rudy wasn't really a Nazi at heart anymore. He explained that a lifetime of consideration had led him to the conclusion that all political movements were pointless, given that the world was secretly controlled by an elite group known as the Illuminati. He shared a few of his opinions in an off-the-cuff sort of way.

A man of medium build, Rudy wore the dark sunglasses and uniform of a chauffeur, right down to the visored cap and black leather gloves. His hands never once left the steering wheel, and he always faced the road. For all his nuttiness, he was the kind of driver who put his passengers at ease.

He made Edmund sit in the back seat, which, in a Cadillac sedan, wasn't generally an unpleasant place to be. There was plenty of legroom and knee clearance, and it even had crafted stitching patterns. There was too much leather, though, for Edmund's taste, and the overpowering smell of it gave him a slight headache, even with the side window open.

After the war, Rudy emigrated from Heidelberg, which he described as a fairy-tale city overlooked by an ancient, red-sandstone castle. During the war, the people of Heidelberg used torches and lights to make the Allied bombers believe the castle was already on fire. This ingenuity spared the structure from the destruction incurred at other ancient landmarks. Every year, Heidelberg celebrated with a Burning of the Castle festival, reenacting the grand event. As with most German festivals, it was largely a socially acceptable excuse for breaking out the Heidelberger Pilsner and getting tight as a tick, according to Rudy.

Edmund had Rudy drop him off at Mort's, which was only two blocks from the apartment.

Edmund bought a can of coconut milk, instant rice, plantains, and some fruit cocktail. He paid for it from the $50 Elon Bennett had given him for consulting on the gardens. *$50*. He could hardly believe it.

Back home, he cooked the rice, and sliced and fried the plantains. Grandam asked about his day. He told her all about the Bennetts, about their spacious house and neglected gardens. When he told her about Rudy and his unusual beliefs, she shook her aged head and said, "It's easier for some to believe they are the victims of greater powers than to assume responsibility for their own actions."

By the time he finished talking about his afternoon, he had mixed the coconut milk in with the rice and served it up with the plantains on terra-cotta plates.

"I got us fruit cocktail for dessert," he said.

As he sat on the loveseat, he was glad to see the television was turned off. On the carpet beside her rocking chair lay of a copy of the novella, *Chronicle of a Death Foretold* by Gabriel García Márquez. Grandam had weak eyes and had all but given up on reading when Edmund learned he could order large-print books for her from the library.

"Older minds need to stay active," he told her, "or they just dry up."

Now she read as much as a book a week. She confessed that sometimes her thoughts wandered when she read, and she sometimes had to go back and reread entire pages, but Edmund reassured her that happened to everyone.

"Tell me about your book, Grandam."

"Well, I'm only about halfway through it. You've read it, Edmund?"

"I read it in high school, but I don't remember much of it."

"It's about love and murder. About jealousy and wicked tongues and shame." She toyed with the heart-shaped pendant she wore around her neck. Edmund had given it to her one year for her birthday. "It's a sad story so far, but well-told."

"Sounds like you're enjoying it."

"I am. You take such good care of me, Edmund. I don't know what I would do without you."

"You never need to worry about that, Grandam."

When they cleaned their plates, he brought out the fruit cocktail in tulip ice-cream dishes.

"Oh, Edmund," she said happily, "you got the kind with the mangoes!"

Little things were what she appreciated.

His heart filled with love for this woman who'd raised him since his parents had died in the car crash, leaving him an orphan at seven years old. Grandam had brought him into her small apartment, never complaining of the burden this must have been for her. He had lived with her ever since. Almost twenty years. He had watched her grow frail and crooked, like some old washerwoman from a storybook, until she retired and her Social Security kicked in. Then it was his turn to take care of her, which he did, unquestioningly.

"Tell me about what our ancestors did to the captured warriors, Grandam."

She scooped the last of her fruit cocktail into her mouth and set the dish on the floor. She smacked her lips. "Well, as you know, the Kai-Tangata were a primitive people, and we viewed enemy flesh as just one more plunder to be shared. Oh, yes, we were savage about it, delighting in the prisoner's torment. We took turns with the dagger, sliced away slowly at skin and muscle, our red-painted faces hovering over our victim like devils from a fiery realm."

Her features turned grim.

"The sweat would pop on the enemy's anguished face as we gradually filled the simmering, earthenware stew pots with the smaller bits, and the roasting grills with the larger ones. Before our prisoner died, he smelled the smoke of his flesh cooking with yams, taro, and wild onions—and sometimes, just before death, when the end was near, we ripped open our enemy's ribs and held up his still-beating heart, for him to see."

Her ancient eyes gleamed.

"The remainder of the flesh we stripped from the bones. We cracked the scraped bones to get at the marrow. The heart and the liver and the kidneys, and long strings of entrails were cleaned, sliced and battered, and all of it was cooked up and served on a table in beds of spiced amaranth leaves, on platters and in coconut shells. The hands and feet were roasted whole and given to the babies to gnaw on. And displayed on the table, in the midst of the feast, sat the severed head of the fallen enemy, the benefactor of the meal, where he or she could observe from the next world as we dined in gluttonous victory.

"After the meal, of course, we had a special use for the head."

Her reference, he suspected, was to the primitive practice of head-shrinking, though she never elaborated.

Edmund collected the dishes and put them in the sink. He sprayed dish soap on them and ran hot water until the basin filled with soapy bubbles. Letting them soak, he put on a pot of coffee. The coffeemaker commenced its gurgling.

"Tell me again, Grandam, how the Kai-Tangata came to leave the island."

She was quiet for a spell, knitting together her thoughts, the caramel-colored contours of her aged face pulled tight in concentration.

He went to the kitchenette and brought back the cups of coffee.

"Unbeknownst to the Kai-Tangata," she said, "our sworn enemies the Koroghori had enlisted the aid of a brutish tribe from a neighboring island. We were foolish. It never occurred to us that the cowardly Koroghori would move against us this way, but even a rabbit can turn ferocious when cornered. And that's the way the Koroghori must have felt."

She lifted the cup and sipped.

"They came in the night. Of course, we had sentries posted at the perimeters of our communal enclaves, but they barely had time to sound an alarm before crashing to the ground. These new foes possessed a weapon the Kai-Tangata were unfamiliar with: long reeds that fired feathered darts dipped in poison. We scrambled in the dark for our arms and ran outside to face our attackers. The night filled with a noise like the beating wings of a parrot. It was the sound of the outliers puffing into their deadly tubes."

She paused, overcome with emotion.

"We took down many of them with our cudgels and bows and spears, but in the end, our village became a slaughter grounds, the huts lit in great pillars of flame, casting their wavering light over the mounds of the dead.

"Only two dozen or so of the Kai-Tangata who fled in the fishing boats escaped with their lives. Mostly women and children. Just like that, our island was lost to us, and we were adrift on the open sea."

Her eyes glistened with tears. Even generations later, this loss still stung.

"Everything we have will be taken from us, Edmund. Never forget that. Some things will be stolen, some will be lost, some will be destroyed. People we know will grow distant, move away, die. Or we'll die. Time is measured largely in loss. Remember that always."

"I will, Grandam."

Chapter Nine

Pamela Bates left the Barrytown Snuggle Inn at 10:27 that night. A male voice issued from her cell phone, which she had on speaker mode, asking her to pick up a pint of Ben & Jerry's Cherry Garcia ice cream on the way home. The non-dairy kind.

"I will if you marry me," she said, walking carefree across the parking lot.

"You strike a hard bargain."

"I only want to make an honest man of you, Jake."

He laughed. "Maybe if you throw in a bag of baked Ruffles, I could be persuaded."

"Hold onto that thought."

She opened the door of her Nissan hatchback and slipped behind the wheel.

"Hurry home," Jake said.

"I'll be there in a flash with your groceries. I love it when you wait up for me."

"Well, it's Friday night."

"It is Friday night. Did you have something in mind for this evening?"

"*May*-be. I might have been thinking of something in particular. If you're not too tired."

She laughed. "Never too tired for you, bae."

"And that's what I love about you."

She laughed again. "Maybe this weekend you could get one of your motorhead friends to fix my back window. It's still stuck open and I'm afraid the backseat will get wet if it rains."

"Remind me, and I'll call Lonny tomorrow."

"Sounds good. See you when I get there. Love you."

"Love you, too."

She clicked off the phone and turned the ignition, her mind perhaps filled with visions of candlelit lovemaking.

From behind, Milo reached out a plastic-gloved hand and covered her mouth. He held a razor-sharp blade to her throat.

"Drive," he said.

> Chapter Ten

Of the two gardens, the idea for the backyard one came first. Edmund was stacking 50-pound sacks of organic fertilizer on the outdoor sales floor at Harbo's Garden Center, wondering whether he should make another attempt to contact MsBathory, when a vision came to him. He pictured a line of similar-sized flagstone pavings wandering from the Bennett's patio area to the gardener's cottage, passing through an arched trellis. He imagined the arch draped in colorful asters and chrysanthemums, bordered by ferns and hostas, by lilies and maybe begonias.

On his lunch hour, he alternated between eating his salad and sketching his idea on the back of a discarded manila envelope at one of the lunchroom tables.

"What's that for, Eddie?" Taylin said around her tuna sandwich. She chewed noisily to the side of her mouth where the chipped tooth lurked.

He had deliberately chosen a table with just one chair pulled up to it in the hopes of discouraging company, but Taylin, true to form, failed to pick up on this polite cue. Instead, she snatched a chair from another table, shoved it close to his, and swung in next to him.

"I'm helping someone design a garden," he said.

"At your grandma's apartment?"

"No. Somewhere else."

"And where's that? The Taj Mahal?"

He blinked at her. He supposed he was being a bit obscure. He'd hoped brevity would discourage conversation, but he could see that was a lost cause. "Minnetonka. For that lady from the other day."

"Lady from the other day?" She wiped her mouth with the back of her hand. "Oh, you mean the old bat in the pants suits?"

"Her name's Adele Bennett."

"So, you're a consultant now."

"Something like that."

Taylin eyed the drawing more closely. "Does she live on the lake?"

"Just off it."

She bit into her sandwich and chewed more thoughtfully, then, "Eddie?"

"What?"

"You wouldn't want to go to a movie with me, would you? My treat."

He was about to say something flip when he saw she was being sincere. He stopped breathing. She brushed back her dark, wiry hair and shook her head slightly, using the gesture to fill his silence.

He stabbed his fork into chunks of lettuce and tomato. "Maybe," he said, at last. "Let me think about it."

He didn't want to hurt her feelings, but there was more to it than that.

He glanced up. His answer seemed to mollify her for the time being.

Folding the drawing and putting it in his back pocket, he turned his attention to Taylin and to his salad. As if for the first time, he listened as she went on about goofy customers and hopeless coworkers. About skinflint management and the long hours she had to work. About how her feet ached at the end of the day.

He listened and ate and nodded sympathetically.

Then a truly horrifying thought occurred to him: What if he did go out with this woman whom he had long considered the bane of his existence—*and what if they had a good time?*

> Chapter Eleven

Milo had been driving all night. The faint light of dawn now limned a far horizon of central Illinois farmland.

He'd stopped at a closed hole-in-the-wall around midnight. A Nissan was parked there, roughly the same year as Pamela's. He'd used the utility knife to switch license plates, though the blade was broken and sticky with blood. Changing the plates may have bought him some time, but he would still have to ditch the car soon.

The events of the night were gloriously fresh in his mind. He'd had to use the duct tape to silence Pamela's cries. Too bad. He would rather have had the peals of her screams wash over his nakedness, mingling with the warmth of her blood and the flecks of her skin. But the torture site was outdoors, and, though it was remote, he couldn't risk the chance her wailing might draw undue attention.

Still, he had enjoyed watching her scream with her eyes.

Outside Clinton, Illinois, he turned onto a gravel side road. Rocks and grit clattered in the wheel wells. He followed the route about two miles until he came to an abandoned church. He braked and pulled in there, parking behind the church, out of view of the road. He wiped the car down for prints, inside and out, grabbed the canvas tote, closed the door, and walked away.

His boot heels dug into the gravel and dust; he was once again on the move.

Baba Yaga had appeared last night. She rose from his throat and his swollen tongue, ripping open his mouth at the hinges and pouring out of him into the moonlit woods. Spilling beside the creek onto the prone and bloody figure that once was Pamela—with her purple ponytail and scrubbed, pink skin, with her long legs and pert, pierced nose—but now was so much more.

He carried remnants of the night in double-bagged plastic in his canvas tote.

After a half-hour of walking, he stepped off the gravel onto the main road and followed it to the first convenience store he came to. Between two gas pumps, he wiped down the utility knife and dropped it into a garbage can. Inside, he bought a disappointing but fresh cup of coffee, a sweet roll, and a road map with some of Pamela's cash.

Outside the store, to one side, was a picnic bench. He sat down and smoothed out the map to study it, sipping the coffee and eating the roll. It looked to be 40 miles west to Champaign. From Champaign, he could catch a Greyhound to Chicago. See what kind of trouble he could get into there.

For now, he needed to put miles between himself and that parked Nissan.

He snagged a ride to just outside Weldon with a chatty customer-service representative named Kathleen something-or-other, a cheery little woman in a carrot-orange sundress and bug-eyed sunglasses. Nowadays, even the most imposing driver gives a hitchhiker a thorough once-over before opening the door to him. But not our Kathleen, who just smiled up at him and let him in. In the ensuing 15 minutes of drive time, give or take, she updated him on the price of corn, the pros and cons of astrology, the frustrations of trying to stick to a diet, and an in-law's recent decision to now identify as gender-neutral.

Milo fed her a tough-luck story and, when she dropped him and his canvas bag off on the shoulder of the road, she slipped him a wrinkled twenty. He thanked her and watched her drive off.

Weldon was a pathetic little farm burg with a population of just over four hundred. *Nothing to see here.* He passed on through.

He had walked a little over two hours when he came to De Land, whose downtown highlights included a water tower, a library, a post office, and a grain elevator. He bought a processed-ham sandwich and a carbonated beverage from Casey's General Store with Kathleen's twenty and found a shady tree across the street to rest under.

He took out his map and studied it while he ate. He estimated he still had about twenty-three miles to go. Too far to walk. He'd have to hitch-it, he guessed. He finished his paltry meal and, getting up, brushed crumbs and dirt from his jeans.

That's when he noticed a silver gasoline-tanker truck stopping at Casey's. The driver, a bearded, twenty-something in a uniform shirt, hopped out of the cab and uncoiled two mammoth black hoses. He connected these to the underground gas-pump reservoirs and began filling them. The truck had a ladder in the rear that led to a platform on the top. Emblazoned on the tanker's side were the words, "DirectChoice Energy, Champaign, Illinois."

When the driver finished filling the reservoirs, he uncoupled the hoses and returned them to the tanker. Then he entered the store. When he returned, he paid no mind to the character in the denim jacket at the rear of the truck, reading a map.

By the time the truck had pulled out of the Casey's General Store parking lot, entered U.S. Highway 72 and begun working through its gears, Milo had wedged himself securely to the platform at the top.

Chapter Twelve

Countess Elizabeth Báthory de Ecsed was a Hungarian aristocrat, circa late-1500s, who tortured and killed an untold slew of local peasant girls with depraved and bloodthirsty cruelty. She often left the torsos or dismembered limbs of her victims lying about her castle or kicked them nonchalantly under a bed. When the smell of decomposition became overwhelming, she had servants drag the offending parts outside where they came to litter the surrounding countryside. Some of the corpses were said to bore her teeth marks.

Shielded by privilege, the countess continued her slaughter for some years before she finally overstepped the bounds of 16th-century decorum by choosing to victimize the daughters of lesser nobility. *Hey, you have to draw the line somewhere.*

One narrative about Elizabeth that Denise especially enjoyed was that the countess bathed in the blood of her victims to keep her flesh supple and young. Though this legend was later debunked, Denise preferred to believe it. What was that journalist's maxim? *Never let the facts get in the way of a good story.*

Denise, lying in bed on a lazy Sunday morning, pictured life as a countess in a castle, waited on by servant girls who attended to her every whim. She would snap her fingers at them and order them around all day. She would stroll her castle grounds, leading on leashes naked men who would move about on their hands and knees. At the end of the day, her servants would pull a fur robe from her shoulders, and she would cross the cool tile of the bathroom floor and tentatively dip her toe into a bathtub filled with peasant girls' blood. Still warm, the way she liked it.

Getting back to those naked men on chains....

She slid her fingers down over the cushion of her belly to the parted mound of moist hair below.

Her cell phone rang.

She picked it up off the bed stand beside her and saw on the display that it was Arminda Larch.

"Hello?" Denise said.

She knew Arminda from grade school, but they had not been close then. Years later, in their junior year of high school, their paths crossed as extras in the school play, *Dracula*. It was a musical version, and they both had walk-on roles as vampiric ghouls during the play's overture. They became fast friends, sharing a love for the grim and the grisly: occult studies, heavy-metal bands, Sam Raimi and Tobe Hooper films, Goth makeup and clothing. Denise was more into the literature of cannibalism, and Arminda's tastes ran more toward extreme-horror novels, but they always had plenty to talk about.

For a while, Denise even suspected that Arminda had a lesbian crush on her, and Denise found herself feeling oddly intrigued by the possibility of pursuing such a relationship. But Arminda hitched up with a stoner named Marvin. Denise and Arminda drifted apart after high school, but reconnected at Denise's mother's funeral.

"Did you hear about Pamela Bates?" Arminda said on the telephone.

"Pamela Bates? Trevor Bates' little sister?"

"Not so little anymore, but yeah. You'll never guess what happened to her."

"What?"

After pausing for effect, Arminda said, "The Butcher got her!"

"The Butcher?"

"The Midwest Butcher. You know, the serial killer."

Denise's jaw dropped. "Are you sure?"

"It's on the morning news. They found her in some podunk town in Illinois, in the woods near a creek."

"Holy shit."

"I know, right? The Butcher sliced her to ribbons. The news report was vague but they mentioned she was missing some internal organs."

"Have you been in touch with her at all?"

"Not really, but I ran into Trevor at the VFW New Year's Eve Party. He was there with Mindy Beekman (that skank!), and he told me Pamela was working in some hotel in Illinois, and she was going out with a nice guy. James, I think it was."

"Pamela Bates." Denise whistled.

"Anyways, thought I'd let you know. You busy today?"

"Not really."

"Want to catch lunch at Chipotle in Maple Grove this afternoon?"

"Why not?"

"Noonish?"

"Sure."

"Okay. See you there." Arminda hung up.

Denise whistled again, the news still unsettling her.

Pamela Bates. Who would have thought?

***

Mrs. Bennett was thrilled with Edmund's sketch for the backyard garden.

"Oh, look, Elon," she said, "*an arched trellis.* What an excellent idea, don't you agree?"

"Very imaginative. I like the way the flowers surround it. Did you have a particular style in mind, Edmund?"

Edmund handed his cell phone to Mr. Bennett.

"These are the models we have on hand at Harbo's. If you don't like any of these, we can order one from an online distributor."

Mr. Bennett thumbed through the images of trellises on the phone while Mrs. Bennett squinted over her husband's shoulder. There were three to choose from. "What do you think, Adele?"

"I like the one with the little cherubs on the arch," she said.

"Well, that settles it." He handed the phone back to Edmund. "Cherubs, it is."

"We can leave it as is," Edmund said. "It comes in white, but I could spray paint it for you. Perhaps a pastel blue or a mauve?"

Mr. Bennett looked to his wife for a decision.

"Let's leave it white for the time being," she said. "Unless you think painting it would protect the wood?"

"It's not made of wood," Edmund said. "It's made of a resin material that holds up well, even in Minnesota winters."

"Then we've made the right decision," Mrs. Bennett said.

Edmund spent the day preparing the soil: tilling and testing the pH balance. For being so near the lake, the Bennett soil was more silty than sandy, which meant it was denser and wouldn't drain well, but it was more nutrient rich. An organic compost would add texture and structure to the soil and increase blooms. If he used about a quarter of the backyard for the garden, and laid the compost a half-inch thick, he estimated the cost to be about $3,000. The trellis would cost another $200, plus delivery. If they balked at the price, he could go down to a quarter-inch on the compost, which would trim that expense to $1,500. If he went with a synthetic fertilizer, he could save more, but synthetic fertilizers had their drawbacks. A pallet of flagstones for the walkway would cost about $300, but shipping would tack on another $1,000. Or he could go with rubber faux stones, which were much lighter. He worked steadily as he did his silent math.

Mrs. Bennett brought a glass of water to him every half-hour or so. "You must keep hydrated, Edmund," she said.

At around noon, he pulled out the hummus and crackers he had picked up from Mort's.

He finished the tilling as dusk approached. After he put away the tools, Mrs. Bennett brought out two glasses of lemonade, and they sat on the front stoop and watched the sun set on Lake Minnetonka. He explained the options for the garden and expected Mrs. Bennett to talk it over at length with her husband, but instead, when she brought the glasses inside and returned, it was with a credit card. "Put all expenses on this card," she said. "Use your best judgment."

She also gave him $200 in cash for the day's work, which he thought was too much, but she insisted he take it.

On the way back, Rudy launched into a diatribe involving, of all things, the Denver International Airport. "If you check out the records, Edmund, you might be surprised to learn that when it was built the airport was more than $2 billion over budget. *$2 billion.* That's massive, even by government standards. But it's a fact. You could look it up. Now I ask you where did that money go?"

"Construction overruns?"

"Yes. Exactly." In the rearview mirror, Edmund could see Rudy's eyes sparkle. "Construction costs. Some say the added construction costs came from building a secret underground bunker."

"Why would they build an underground bunker at an airport?"

"Some would argue, to house the North American headquarters of the Illuminati."

Why would anyone argue that? Edmund was afraid to ask. "Hmmm," he said, noncommittally.

At Mort's, Edmund, flush with the cash the Bennetts had paid him, ordered from the deli: three-bean salad, candied sweet potatoes, and for dessert a rice pudding. *Grandam will be pleased*, he thought.

However, when he entered the apartment with the deli goodies, Grandam met him at the door and hugged him. "Oh, Edmund. I'm afraid I have bad news."

He set the grocery bag on the sink counter. "What is it, Grandam?"

She pulled back, but held onto his shoulders. "Do you remember Pamela Bates?"

"Trevor Bates' sister?" Trevor and Edmund had been on the Cooper High basketball team together. Though, in truth, Edmund had spent much of the season warming the bench. Trevor was an excellent shooting guard, a maniac on the court, and was always friendly to Edmund. Trevor went on to play at Mankato State University for a year before tearing a ligament in his knee, ending any hope of a pro career.

"She's been killed."

"Killed?" *Poor Trevor and his family. They must be heartsick.*

"You know that Butcher fellow they're always talking about?"

69

"The Midwest Butcher killed her?"

At ten o'clock, the news offered up some details on the Midwest Butcher's slaying of 22-year-old Pamela Bates, a former resident of New Hope, Minnesota. KARE-11 anchor Julie Nelson gave a summary of the crime. "A woman walking her dog this morning along a creek in Fairview Garden Park, just outside Barrytown, Illinois, found Pamela—or what remained of her—slaughtered, naked, and missing several body parts. Police believe the killer fled in the victim's car, and they have issued an all-points bulletin for the vehicle, an early-model Nissan Versa hatchback." Julie gave the plate number.

The screen displayed a yearbook picture of Pamela, smiling brightly with braces on her teeth. Edmund thought he recognized her from the attendees of the basketball games, but he couldn't be sure. He wasn't even sure he knew her other than by name.

"You should go to the funeral," Grandam said. "For Trevor's sake."

"Yes. Of course."

Chapter Thirteen

L eave it to Mindy Beekman to show up at her boyfriend's sister's wake wearing a cardinal-red mini-skirt with a plunging neckline and a matching red, wide-brimmed hat.

Give her credit, at least, for wearing a veil on the hat, even if it was a red veil.

Denise, in one of her tastefully glum black dresses, nodded to Mindy and shook just the fingers of her extended hand. Denise provided Mindy a soulful expression and quickly moved past to Trevor.

Behind her, Arminda offered Mindy a clumsy curtsy, then moved on without stopping. Arminda wore a charcoal-gray pants suit, sparing all the embarrassment of her preternaturally white legs.

"Hello, Denise," Trevor said. "Thank you for coming." He looked exhausted, and she saw the beginnings of crow's feet at the corners of his eyes. She also spotted a touch of gray at his temples. Still, Trevor had retained his handsome features and athletic build. He wore a muted-blue, notched-lapel suit, single-breasted. His trousers bore razor-sharp creases.

What did this man see in a clueless goof like Mindy Beekman?

She hugged Trevor. "I'm so sorry about Pamela." And she sincerely was.

"Not too many people from the old neighborhood around here anymore. Most of them left New Hope for greener pastures."

"Well, it looks like she had a lot of friends."

Trevor scanned the crowd with searching eyes. "I don't even know most of these people. Rubberneckers are my guess. Just want to say they went to the funeral of one of the Midwest Butcher's victims. At least they're being respectful. I'm hoping they don't get it into their minds to start stealing souvenirs."

She hugged him again and moved on to the next phase of the reception line: the parents. Mrs. Bates had yet to cry herself out but was getting there, dabbing at her eyes with a satin handkerchief. Mrs. Bates recognized Denise, but not Arminda, who Denise introduced as one of Pamela's friends from school. Mr. Bates, looking somewhat disheveled, shook the girls' hands absent-mindedly. He wore a Navy-blue suit that was a size too small.

Behind him, Pamela's boyfriend, Jake Hanson, looked lost and unsure of himself. Denise recognized him from a newspaper photo.

"She was a special girl," Denise said to him. He looked at her as if she were speaking a foreign language. Impulsively, she hugged him. The poor guy looked like he needed one.

The casket, a stainless steel model, was closed (for obvious reasons). A simple bouquet of white roses decked the casket's center. Denise preferred the old, six-sided coffins to modern caskets, which she considered behemoth and impersonal by comparison. Old-style coffins were richer in tradition, mystery and superstition. Besides, they always reminded her a little of daguerreotypes of Old West outlaws propped up in displays of death. She made a mental note to include a rider in her will that she be buried in a six-sided coffin.

Actually, she preferred the idea of drifting off on a flaming raft like the Vikings of yore, but imagined that would be illegal and, in any case, impractical.

Pamela, the obituary said, would be interred tomorrow at Gethsemane Catholic Cemetery.

Arminda, still clinging to her religion's trappings, knelt before the casket, made the sign of the cross, and muttered a prayer. When she was done, the girls moved to the first of three easels exhibiting snapshots of Pamela in various stages of life: as a baby, as a toddler, as a young schoolgirl, as a teenager, as an adult woman, and that's where it ended. A life tragically cut short.

Denise was in one of the photos: the birthday party for Trevor. The one where Momma Rat munched down her offspring. Denise looked like a doofus in her frilly party dress.

Having signed the attendance book and visited with everyone they recognized, Denise and Arminda were leaving through the funeral home's antechamber when, in through the front door, walked a faintly familiar face: a caramel-skinned boy, vaguely equatorial in ancestry. Denise didn't know his name and doubted they had ever met before, but when his eyes fell on her, he looked as if a thunderbolt had struck him.

Cautiously, he made his way toward her, the sleeves of his suit coat slightly too short for his long, slender arms, his jet hair held back with some product, his dark eyes fixed on her. Approaching her, she expected him to open with a bland greeting of some kind.

He whispered into her ear with the prodding lilt of a gentle inquiry, "Ms. Bathory?"

Chapter Fourteen

From AnthraxBordello in Friendship, Maine, a dentist: "Every time I look into someone's mouth now, I think of you, Raoul. As I work a crown into place, drill out a cavity, or bond a chipped tooth, I imagine what it would feel like to fall into your open mouth. To feel the sting of your sharp canines and incisors, and the grinding of your molars as you reduce my flesh to a paste. As the wash of your saliva carries me down the moist tunnel of your throat. My essence would live on inside you, I am sure. These thoughts sometimes arouse me, sometimes to the point of orgasm, my soft whimpers of ecstasy barely hidden from the patient and my assistant by the wet *woosh* of my suction aspirator or the pulsing whir of my steely drill."

***

Yegor Dzhurmongaliev (a.k.a. George) peered out the window of his writing den with his one good eye and noticed that someone had freshly tilled a sizeable section of the Bennetts' backyard. *What were they planting back there? Flowers, probably.*

Back in Chicago, in the tiny backyard of their two-story brownstone, George's mother had kept a garden. In that plot, Mamushka grew beets, cabbage, potatoes, onions, and small cucumbers, which she made into pickles. Her petite garden was quite prolific, and what they didn't eat straight from the soil, she canned in mason jars and stored in a back-porch pantry for later.

He especially loved her homemade bread-and-butter pickles.

Like the Bennetts', his was a backyard flower garden. Bedraggled, true, but a flower garden all the same. Minnesota perennials, mostly: Shasta daisies, coneflowers, speedwell, daylilies. He liked to think that what he lacked in gardening talent, he made up for in enthusiasm and sheer love for the blooms.

If he only had the time to devote to his flowers. After he finished this book, he told himself. It was, after all, nearly done. But then, of course, there would be another book.

Or would there?

Maybe this one would be his last.

A graduate in Slavic languages from Columbia University, he had made his reputation as a respected translator and writer. He had already fashioned a prolific legacy of more than 30 written and translated works.

He'd won the Rossica Prize for his translation of *Slovo o polku Igoreve (The Song of Igor's Campaign)* and was short-listed for his collection of 17th-century poems by Russian women (*Elderberry Incantations*). His biography of Tsarevna Natalya Alexeyevna (*Playwright, Reformer, and Sister to the Tsar*) received a PEN award and was nominated for a Pulitzer. Additionally, he'd translated Fonvizin's satirical comedies (with critiques), an anthology of *bylina* epic poems, and three volumes of early-Slavic oral history gathered from interviews, diaries, and obscure publications.

But this new volume was taking more out of him than anything he'd done previously. And it wasn't just old age and poor health—he was almost ninety years old—slowing him down, though these were factors.

Besides having only one working eye, George was troubled by pseudogout, which was like regular gout except it only flared up every four or five years. Oddly enough, this rare occurrence was a chief disadvantage of pseudogout. Because it cropped up so rarely, it wasn't rendered a nonfactor by regular, proactive doses of medicine. Instead, those with pseudogout suffered a week or two of often intense pain until the indomethacin pills eventually kicked in.

Then they were left alone until the condition once again ambushed them four or five years down the road.

As fate would have it, he was currently in the midst of the most painful phase of a flare-up.

George's condition concentrated in his right big toe, which was swelled like a plum. It was so exceedingly sore that even the minor pressure of a bed sheet on the toe was unbearable. His shoe no longer fit over his swollen joint, so he was resigned to limping about in fuzzy black slippers, even in public. This distracted him from his work. Or maybe the ailment was his body's way of telling him: *don't go back there.*

Writing and researching this book took him to a very dark place. It was like crawling down a rat hole. He had always felt a sense of metamorphosis when submerged in his work, but this project took him far deeper into realms he did not want to visit. He returned from these mental sojourns feeling unclean. Tainted even.

George hobbled across a patterned Persian throw rug to his writing desk, the only piece of furniture in which he took any real pride. Its massive mahogany surface, finished in black lacquer and gilded in gold, was a blizzard of stacked books collected from his walls of bookshelves, assorted correspondences, and paperwork. Amid this deluge sat his trusty Toshiba laptop computer.

He pulled up a straight-back wooden chair and reluctantly picked up the thread of his writing from where he left off.

This was his second book on Baba Yaga, the Russian witch who decided case-by-case whether to help or to kill (and eat) those who knocked at her door. His first volume was a translation of folktales for the University of Minnesota Press. He'd spent a year collecting obscure Cyrillic texts and painstakingly converting them to English. The tales often overlapped one another, and all had multiple versions. Splicing these stories into self-contained segments had required dexterity, both as a translator and a writer. The finished product, *Russian Wonder Tales of Baba Ya*ga, was well-received, not on the scale of an Andreas Johns or a Vladimir Propp work perhaps, but was a scholarly and critically acclaimed translation nonetheless.

Shortly after the publication of this first book, he received an invitation from the office of His Holiness Patriarch Kirill, primate of the Russian Orthodox Church in Moscow, to peruse some ancient writings on the subject of Baba Yaga recently uncovered in the church's scholarly library. Unable to resist such an offer, George had flown to Moscow as soon as arrangements could be made, and was surprised to find handwritten, often copiously illustrated, pages upon pages of legible documents, tracing as far back as 800 CE. Some were in the form of parchment scrolls, and some were even in lead casts of engraved Cyrillic cuneiforms. The lead tablets were copies, he was sure, but exquisite ones.

He was barred from removing any of the texts from the library but was free to study them, copy them by hand, photograph them and scan them into his computer, which he did, backing up these files daily to a cloud drive.

He spent three months' worth of ten- and twelve-hour days in a dusty back room of the scholarly library poring over this tantalizing collection, which traced the legend of Baba Yaga to its most primitive roots. Some of the texts were so ancient that all he could do was copy them until he had a chance to decipher them back home where he had access to his personal collection of obscure translation guides.

When he finished, he discussed his preliminary findings with His Holiness Patriarch Kirill and ranking church officials at a modest dinner held in his honor, before returning to Minnetonka to begin work on the project in earnest. That was more than a year and a half ago.

George winced as he accidentally knocked his sore toe against a chair leg.

He learned from the oldest manuscripts that Baba Yaga had once been worshiped by proto-Slavic cannibal cults who dwelled in forests and swamps in the area of what is now western Poland to the Dnieper River in Belarus. By some accounts, Baba Yaga was the mother of Svantovit, the four-headed god of war, and Perun, the thunder god. That her myth outshined her offsprings' was a testament to her staying power, much of which was fueled by the raw horror she uniquely evoked.

Even in modern versions, Baba Yaga was a terrifying figure, given to deadly rages and to feasting on the flesh of the young. But the original version of this demon was much worse, George discovered. Here she was the very essence of wickedness and evil, and those who worshiped her engaged in practices that might have made an ancient Aztec blanch.

Woe to the wanderers, captive warriors or other foreigners who wound up in the clutches of the dreaded Azhbaguls, the Zhodislavas or the Gostrados. They would be fattened on lard, gristle, suet, and meat marble until the next sacrificial festival. Then one of them would be led away into a specially dedicated, underground chancel and....

Consulting his notes, George began to peck at the keyboard:

With an idol of their powerful goddess looking on, the priests in ceremonial hoods tied the wrists and ankles of their human sacrifice in knots of coarse rope, while they whispered spells.

"We, the Old Believers, celebrate the forbidden one and the power she has wielded since the days of our ancestors' ancestors, whose names we still revere."

The poor wretch, naked and stretched on a curved stone altar, watched as the priests held up sleek and deadly obsidian knives and swords. The surfaces of the blades crawled with etchings of furious Baba Yagas that gleamed in the light of a hundred torches. The pommels of the blades were elongated, glaring skulls.

Around and around the prone offering, the priests paraded with their knives and swords, striking ceremonial poses that elicited roars from the crowd.

One priest drew a flaming brand from the assemblage and shook it at the captive wretch, its fire giving off smoke and sparks. Slowly, he lowered it toward the figure's stomach until the flesh began to sizzle.

The convulsions of the victims' limbs were greeted with chants of "Baba Yaga, bony leg! Fly to us, your sons and daughters!" This chanting melded with the cries of anguish and the steady pounding of ritual drums.

George looked up, pausing in his typing. He became lightheaded.

The drumming, the chanting, the screams of the tortured had become almost real to him. It was as if this dark world, this morbid past gleaned from the scribblings of savages centuries ago, was claiming him somehow, as one of its own. Though it terrified him, he was loath to fight the plunge because his immersion in this other world brought a crisp insight to his vision and writing.

Some outward power seemed to take over his fingers. He typed on:

"Baba Yaga, bring rain to our fields!" the throng chanted. "Make us strong and fierce!"

A trio of hooded figures approached, clutching cudgels formed from the shoulder blades of snow rams. These they rained down on the offering, splitting and bruising skin, cracking bones, *chug-chug-chug*, in time with the ritual drumming.

"Bony leg, protect us from enemies within and without!"

Now a priest appeared with a steaming ladle of molten lead.

The naked figure, still twitching from the burns inflicted by the torch and the blows struck down by the skeletal clubs, looked up in horror as the ladle slowly dipped. It was the last time the miracle of sight would unfold in this unfortunate's muddled mind. The molten lead gushed into the sockets of the wretch's eyes, and the poor creature's animal-like howls filled the air in the squat chancel like a tempest rising. It whistled in the congregants' ears, some of whom dropped to their knees, some of whom reached their fists skyward. Some twirled with the roar of the torrent. Some beat at their chests. All became seized in the throes of ethereal ecstasy.

"Baba Yaga, fly to us! Fly to us! Fly to...."

George's voice joined the chanting.

Along with the other worshipers, he now felt the presence of the unholy goddess scowling at them from the hollow haunts of the afterworld.

George watched the priests flay the sufferer with their obsidian swords and knives, sharp as surgical steel. When at last the victim perished, they decapitated the corpse, and expertly sliced away the warm flesh from the skull and scooped out the brains. They carved holes in the temples, through which they ran a wooden pole already racked with dozens of other skulls. They hung the post on the sanctum wall, where it joined its grinning brethren by the hundreds.

The priests flung the decapitated body to the ground and fell upon it with their sharp blades. They deftly butchered the meat from the bones and handed it out to the supplicants, who wolfed down the bloody strips, awash in the presence of their Baba Yaga, who smiled on them with metallic teeth from her chthonic brink.

And George was there among the writhing horde, reaching out for his own taste of flesh.

Chapter Fifteen

I t was one of the few times in her life that Denise was at a loss for words.

"Come again?" she said at last.

"I never expected to run into you this way," the slender man said, offering his hand. "Did you know Pamela?"

"You have me mistaken for someone else." She took his hand anyway and gave it a robotic squeeze. The skin of his fingers was warm against hers.

"I was on the basketball team with Trevor. The Cooper Hawks. It's such a tragedy about Pamela, don't you think?"

Arminda milled close, as if sensing there was something curious about this encounter.

"Forgive me. I'm Edmund." Edmund eyed her quizzically.

"I'm Denise," she said automatically. This Edmund guy had knocked her for a loop. *How did he know about Ms. Bathory?* A chilliness flowered up her spine. *He was one of them. One of the freaks from the website!*

"Very nice meeting you. I hope we see each other again." He smiled at her absently, nodded to Arminda, and strolled off into the crowded antechamber.

***

"How's it going, cowboy?" The speaker in the uptown roadhouse had some skin condition, psoriasis or eczema; Milo always got those two confused. Nothing as severe as what his father had; just a light frosting on the brow and chin. The fellow's eyes were a warm, robin's-egg blue, and he had puffy, pink lips.

"My name's Bill Griggs," Milo said, "but my friends call me Buster."

"Henry Kowarski. My friends call me Hank."

When they shook hands, Milo detected the soft, moist grip of someone socially awkward. Maybe the skin rash made Hank self-conscious. Or maybe he was another of life's lonely souls.

Milo let Hank buy him a beer.

Since arriving in Chicago, Milo had drifted from one seedy motel to another. He supported himself by selling plasma at a donation site on West 87th Street, working a part-time, day-labor job at a sheet-metal manufacturing plant, and taking handouts from people like pimply faced Hank. Already this urban lifestyle was getting old. It was just about time to blow the Windy City, maybe swing over to Iowa or up to Wisconsin.

"I'm a union carpenter," Hank said. "What's your line, Buster?"

"I was a realtor, but the firm went belly up. It's been a rough couple of months. Got some savings to carry me through, though, until I settle on something new."

"Still looking to work in real estate?"

"I don't know. Maybe. If I can catch on somewhere, sure. The money's good."

"You from Chi-Town?"

Hank kept asking questions, and Milo kept dishing out lies. Then they talked about the Bears and the Cubs. Hank did most of the talking on these subjects since Milo knew little about sports, but Milo could tell Hank was uncomfortable in the role of a talker. He was more the listening type.

"I've got an autographed jersey of Jim McMahon at my house," Hank said. There was an uneasy silence. Then he added, "If you'd like to see it."

"Your house?"

"Sure. Why not?"

Milo drained his beer. "Why not, indeed?"

Hank drove a Chevy Tahoe, metallic black, with all the extras: 10-inch touchscreen, stereo sound system, keyless entry, automatic windows, blind-spot monitoring. Roomy. Milo stretched his legs in the passenger seat. The Tahoe sailed down the asphalt and concrete roadways of a glittery night, engine humming like a bumblebee.

"Nice ride, Hank."

"What do you drive?"

"F-150," Milo said without a pause, "but I loaned it to a friend of mine who's moving."

Hank turned on the radio. Keith Urban, "Days Go By." *Yes, they do, if you're lucky.*

Hank lived in Schaumburg, a northwestern suburb, home of what was once the world's largest shopping center, Woodfield Mall, still the largest in Illinois. Schaumburg was also home to the intriguingly named Wood Library-Museum of Anesthesiology, which Milo decided he really must visit one of these days.

The condominium was about a thousand square feet. Plush carpeting and gray hardwood floors, flat eggshell walls, modular furnishings, and glass-fronted cabinetry. A corner curio displayed bowling trophies and artifacts of the Jewish religion. Curtained windows opened onto a view of a pond, its night-blackened surface milky with streaks of distant arc lights.

"You like living by yourself?" Milo asked, turning from the window. His head was growing foggy, and he felt himself slipping in and out of a familiar trance. His goddess was getting restless again.

"Sometimes. Want a beer?"

"Sure."

"Maybe a little weed?"

"Why not?"

They sat on a leather sofa, nursing their beers, puffing on a hand-rolled cigarette. Hank told him a story about a guy at work who fired a nail gun into a wooden plank, but for some reason, the plank was hollow, and the nail jetted through the board, ricocheted off a lunch pail and took out a cardinal in a shower of crimson feathers. The beer and the smoke wormed their way into Milo's brain through the neurons and glial cells, and, for a moment, all he could see were sparks of light and the image of the bird exploding.

His perceptions wavered from light to dark. His face and fingers went alternately numb and tingly. Sound faded in and out. Awareness bent and reflected through a stratum of flickering cognizance. He would be looking to his left, and the next thing he knew he was facing right. Now he was laughing; now he was solemn. It reminded him of a strobe light, only with illuminations that grew gradually more intense.

What was in this weed?

Then he realized it wasn't the weed. It was Baba Yaga, working her way out. Her twisted nails scratched in his innards.

Not yet. Not yet. *Let me have my fun first.* But he had already lost control of himself.

His eyes watered at the brilliance of Hank looking concerned, Hank looking aroused, Hank kissing him, Hank pulling off Milo's denim jacket.

All the while, she was clawing up inside him, from the pit of his stomach, through his organs and muscles and corded veins, into the vertebrae and viscera of his neck. Her fingernails poked up from the back of his throat and scraped the roof of his mouth. And somewhere in the blank spaces between the blinding flashes, Baba Yaga got loose.

It all played out in a panorama of sheeted light and fathomless dark.

Hank falling, a gash on his forehead spilling blood, bruising; Hank on the plush carpet, crab crawling backward, eyes full and shiny as silver dollars; Hank collapsing from his elbows, his nose mushy and at an angle.

Milo rained down blow after blow, pummeling the carpenter's flesh and bones until his clenched fists throbbed. Pounding away the carpenter's stubbornly clinging life.

Suddenly all resistance ceased. Hank's eyes rolled back and went glassy. His plump bottom lip was torn from his face, exposing a death's head grimace of crooked incisors and bloody gums.

And Milo, sitting astride Hank's stomach, chewed contentedly.

Chapter Sixteen

Movie night went more smoothly than Edmund had foreseen, which made things thornier for him.

Taylin picked him up outside the apartment building at eight o'clock for the nine o'clock showing of a *Fast & Furious* flick. Her car was a white sedan with a hint of rust along the passenger-side rocker panel. When he slid in, he was immediately immersed in Taylin World. Her steering wheel was shiny pink and shaped like a heart. Her rearview mirror dangled a glittery swan-shaped ornament, and butterflies the color of grape jelly took wing on ebony floor mats below.

The trace of orange-scented perfume he detected came from Taylin herself, who, by the dashboard lights, admittedly approximated a look of sexy allure. He'd never seen her wear makeup at Harbo's, but now she wore a shimmer of pink on her lips and a pale dusting of cornflower blue on her eyelids. Her brown-black hair was pinned back with thin gold barrettes, and a gold choker chain rested at the base of her neck. A loose and silky floral blouse sheathed her barrel body, and she wore faux-leather, cropped culottes.

"You look nice," he said, shutting the door.

Her face went blank for a moment as if shaken by the compliment. She gave him a twitchy smile, engaged the transmission, and drove off into the night.

The movie was alright. The special effects and action scenes were engaging, but he had difficulty following the storyline, and between car chases, his mind kept wandering back to the funeral.

He'd never before met anyone from the dark web in real life, as far as he knew. But there was no question: Denise Nils was the haunting, naked, blood-drizzled woman from the Forlorn Flesh Fetishist. After the wake, he had found her picture in his Cooper High yearbook, and another of her in a cast photo from the musical, *Dracula*, which he remembered seeing with Grandam. That night Grandam had worn the heirloom brooch her mother had given her for special occasions.

The picture from the play was more in keeping with the Ms. Bathory persona, but her official school photo also had a definite Goth vibe.

Should he try to contact her again? *Would that be creepy?*

Then there was the matter of the orange-scented, popcorn-munching femme beside him in the theater's dark. He glanced at her now and then, careful not to let her catch him looking. Her profile, limned by the light from the movie screen, appeared almost delicate. She ate the popcorn one kernel at a time, masticating thoughtfully, her gaze fixed straight ahead.

She still called him Eddie all evening, but somehow it didn't bother him like it usually did. (What was happening to him?)

And then there was his flower garden. Technically it was the Bennetts' garden, but somewhere in its planning and realization, it had become his, as well. Conceptually his, anyway. In that sense, it had become part of him, as native as the sensation of air flowing in and out of his lungs.

Or maybe he had become a part of the garden. An organic extension of the soil, roots and blooms.

What was that quote from the Buddha?

"He who experiences the unity of life sees his own self in all beings, and all beings in his own self, and looks on everything with an impartial eye."

He wasn't sure about that last part, but the rest explained his feelings on gardening to a tee.

While his eyes focused on the fluttering images on the screen, in his mind he pictured himself groping in the dirt, saw the trellis and the stone walkway he'd yet to install, saw the Bennetts smiling and nodding at him from the shade of their patio, sipping cold drinks.

When Taylin finished her popcorn, she set down the empty bag, reached over, and covered his hand on the armrest. The skin of her fingers was soft. He had to admit, it felt good being here with her, handholding in the dark of Willow Creek Theater.

Would Denise ever want to hold my hand?

When Taylin dropped him off after the film, they hugged, and she pecked him on the cheek. *Another barrier crossed.*

Edmund was relieved when he entered the apartment to find Grandam still awake, watching a rerun of an old private-eye show. *Mannix*, maybe. He did not want to be alone just then with his thoughts, and he wasn't sure he had the concentration to clear his mind on his own.

"How was the movie?" she asked.

"Oh, you know, a lot of squealing tires and car chases."

"How did your date go?"

Edmund tilted his hand from side to side in a so-so gesture. "How was your evening?"

"Better than yours, apparently. You look paler than that time I saved you from the crocodile."

This cheered him a bit, this inside joke. When he first came to stay with her, he had noticed a crocodile-skin suitcase under her bed and asked about it.

"When you were a baby, a crocodile crawled up from the sewers and threatened to attack you," she had said, adopting a theatrical manner. "So, I wrestled him to his back, pinned him, and had a suitcase made out of him. To teach him that no crocodile was going to eat my little Edmund."

Even at seven, he knew this was a joke, but it made him laugh during a sad time in his life.

"I finished reading the Márquez book," Grandam now said, "which left me feeling pensive."

"I'm feeling a bit pensive myself."

"The girl?"

"I'm not sure how to feel about her. I never really even liked her that much before. Now I kind of do. I don't know. She calls me Eddie."

Grandam chuckled.

"And there's another girl I met who I think I have more in common with. But I'm not sure if she'd be interested in me."

"Affairs of the heart can be tricky. Especially at your age."

"Do you want any more coffee?"

"No. I think I'm just going to fall asleep here in front of the TV, watching an old show."

Edmund unplugged the coffeemaker, poured himself a cup and sat on the loveseat.

"Help me get my mind off these women, Grandam. Tell me a little about how the Kai-Tangata came to New Guinea."

She pinched the bridge of her nose, and her eyes took on that faraway look. She absentmindedly lifted the remote from her lap and muted the volume.

"Well, the two dozen or so Kai-Tangata who escaped the island in fishing boats sailed for days across the Coral Sea. We knew we could never go back. Fishers had stocked the boats with fresh water, but only enough for only a day or so, so we had to ration carefully. The sea was full of parrotfish, groupers and cods, which we caught in our nets and ate raw.

"I'm not sure why we settled on the jungle shoreline of what was then Dutch South New Guinea. It wasn't the first landfall we spotted, and every day on the boats diminished our supply of water, but something about that land drew us.

"The jungle, I suppose. It reminded us of our beloved island, but that was only part of it.

"Fate commanded our presence on that soil, and who were we to deny destiny?

"And so we up settling there. Starting over. Mostly women and children, but a few men as well. We fished, hunted, gathered papaya, mangos, and golden apples. And, of course, we brought the old ways with us, capturing and feeding on our new enemies.

"Over time, we migrated farther into the leafy jungle, where we multiplied and over the years broke off into clans known as the Marind Anims, better known to western Europeans as the Cannibal Gardeners."

Chapter Seventeen

M ilo was one of seven children, growing up in what was once called the Bronzeville district of Milwaukee. Initially settled by Germans and Eastern European Jews, by the time Milo came along, the area was more ethnically mixed and had already begun its tragic erosion into poverty and neglect. Today the area is known as Triangle North, one of the city's most crime-ridden neighborhoods.

Milo's father, a skinny little Greek immigrant with a predilection for Evan Williams whiskey, was an auto mechanic, though he often went a year or more between jobs. Stavros Castellanos, known to his drinking buddies as Stash, was a big Milwaukee Brewers fan. During jobless summers, the games constantly played on the living room TV or his transistor radio. He used to joke he only needed his wife to pump out two more ankle-biters, and he could field a team.

To his children, Stash was, for the most part, a sort of ghost figure. A boozy, shadowy presence that drifted through their lives without ever really touching them. Sometimes he was home at night, and sometimes he was gone for days. He was really more a boarder than a father to them.

Except when he got his rashes. Then a bizarre change came over him.

Sometimes the creams and ointments helped enough to avert disaster, but usually not. Usually, Daddy wound up sulking and drunk in the house, scratching like mad, and the children scrambled to stay out of his stumbling path.

Milo's father had a chronic inflammatory skin condition in which the blood vessels of his cheeks and nose would redden brightly. Then the skin would break out in weeping papules and pustules. This happened three or four times a year, sometimes lasting weeks, itching and burning terribly. When it passed, it always left on Daddy's face some freshly scarred tracing of its visit. And, on his children, scars of another kind.

Not one to endure such attacks gracefully, at each onset Daddy went harder than normal for the Evan Williams, hard enough to gradually transform himself into another person entirely.

This other Stash was a mean one, given to rages. Quick to cuff, unbearably sharp with his tongue. At times, his eyes shined wildly over the scarlet swath that crawled crazily across his face.

Milo learned to spot the early signs of the skin eruptions. The slightest flush of pink on Daddy's cheeks was cause for alarm. Sometimes Milo could see it coming before his mother could, but when they both saw it, their gaze would lock in a silent acknowledgment. *Here we go again.*

The other Stash was bossy and demanding, barking orders in slurred speech, calling Milo and his brothers "stupid" or "lazy;" Milo's sisters were "ugly" and "sluts." He became progressively freer with his hands, slapping and punching his children on whims. Milo's mother—a flustered, mousey type, Egyptian born, who worked as a cashier at the local Walgreens—would try to calm him down in her panicky voice. But her attempts were largely fruitless, and many were the times she went to work with nasty bruises under her makeup.

He shook the babies, broke Milo's brother's arm, chased his kids around the house, drunkenly clenching a rolled-up newspaper or a baseball bat. "I'm going to kill you!" he shouted, as if it were a cry for rescue from the torments of his flesh. "I'm going to kill all you little bastards!" as if it were a heartfelt appeal to whatever gods may be.

They scattered under beds, hid in closets, ran out into the street with nowhere to go—anything to get away from the maniac with the oozing red rash of his face.

One night he knocked Milo unconscious with a chair. When he awoke, his father was savagely sodomizing his mother in the center of the living room, with his brothers and sisters looking on and crying from the doorways of their bedrooms. Something twisted and wrenched inside Milo that night, and he lost a piece of himself.

That summer, Milo turned eleven and began hurting animals.

Down the block off an alley was a backyard dog who barked insanely whenever someone walked too close to the wire fence. Milo took to taunting the creature, a mutt boxer with cropped ears. Milo would lunge toward the fence, acting as if to jump over it, driving the boxer psycho. The cur would froth at the mouth and snap jaws at the air, while Milo shook with laughter.

One day he approached the mutt, carrying a large brick. When the boxer flew to the fence, Milo brought down the brick with both hands on the crown of the creature's head. The bone buckled, and the boxer fell to the ground, whimpering, eyes glazing, legs convulsing in spasms.

Not so threatening now, are you, you little bastard?

That summer, he hung a kitten, set fire to a collie, stomped a frog to death, and cut the throat of a sweet-tempered terrier. Sometimes at night, in the bed he shared with a brother, he would think about these crimes, and it was during these times he first felt the swell of an erection.

When the school year was about to begin, Milo ran away from home. He headed for the rail yards and rode between the wheels of a piggybacked trailer all the way to St. Paul, Minnesota, armed with only a jackknife, a Zagnut bar, and a flinty determination.

He spent two years in St. Paul, living on the streets and occasionally in shelters where he lied to explain his status, and where they were forever pushing on him resources for runaways in which he had no interest. He learned to eat what he could find, wash up in gas-station bathrooms, panhandle and steal. He turned his first trick in an alley off West Seventh Street, and the hardest part of it was to keep himself from biting off the john's manhood. He broke into buildings, especially in winter months, which are so bone-chilling in the upper north that homeless people sometimes freeze to death.

A kindly old girl found him shivering one night on her enclosed porch. She invited him in, gave him a hot meal, let him shower in her bathroom, let him sleep in her guestroom. After a week of pleasant banter and much Jesus talk, she suggested he turn himself in to authorities, so he might get placement in a foster home. He said he would think about it.

That night, he snuck into her bedroom and stabbed her in the throat with his pocketknife.

She struggled, clawing at the open wound on her neck, her fingers slippery with blood. She looked at him as if seeing him for the first time. Her breath grew ragged and the breach in her throat bubbled. She stopped her clutching. A light in her eyes blinked off, and she lay completely still.

At the moment, Milo had an orgasm.

The day after he killed her, he returned to her room and played with her as if she were a doll. He wiped away the blood and changed the bedding, then he took off her clothes, examined her naked parts, sat her upright, bent her over the bedside, and entered her. He worked a slip over her, laid her back down, and cracked a window to let in a stream of cold air. To help preserve her.

He lived in the house with the old girl's corpse upstairs for more than a week, eating his way through the food in her pantry, watching TV, gathering his strength.

One night he was on her couch, watching a documentary on Jeffrey Dahmer, his Milwaukee homey. They were interviewing a cop who had been in Dahmer's apartment.

Dead-faced, the cop recounted, "There were slices of biceps, thighs, and hearts wrapped in plastic in the refrigerator and the freezer. There were over a dozen human skulls. Dahmer had stripped them of skin and spray-painted some of them. In jars filled with acetone, we found a head, hands, and assorted genitals. All were part of his elaborate fantasy world. Killing and raping these people, you see, was only the beginning for Dahmer."

Only the beginning.

An urge rose darkly in Milo, like a bubble lifting thickly through crude oil. The ascending bubble shook loose the dark framework at his core, and he felt himself coming undone. A leathery, reptilian lust seized him.

In a daze, he went to the kitchen, opened the cutlery drawer, withdrew the longest, sharpest knife he could find, and went upstairs.

Chapter Eighteen

George's eyes snapped open.

Not again.

He was lying facedown on his keyboard in his writing den, arms dangling at his sides.

He sat up too suddenly and banged his foot against a desk leg, sending a shock of pain up his thigh.

Damn pseudogout.

Feeling hemmed in by darkness, he turned on the desk lamp.

How long had he been out this time? The computer clock read 11:29 p.m. Had he been gone five hours? *Gone where?*

The last of the dream still clung to him: the clopping hooves of the red horse barreling toward him through the fog; the red Cossack glaring at him, torch bright as the noonday sun. In the background, thinly rendered in the mist, was the great square house, rotating slowly.

He wiped cold sweat from his brow, and drool from the corner of his lip. He felt as if he was hungover: head pounding, stomach queasy.

There on the computer screen were, once again, words he didn't remember typing. The word count up to 70,626. A chill ran through him. He looked at his writing journal and saw the last word count he had entered was 61,664. That was from this morning's session.

George scrolled up the screen, hoping to find chunks of gibberish, pages full of zzzzzz and cccccccccc left from where he'd rolled on the keys in his sleep. But what met his gaze was page after page of polished writing in his familiar style. And he had no recollection of typing any of it.

He saved and closed the file. For an instant, he considered deleting it. But, frightened as he was, he needed to see this project through to the end.

To the very end.

He stared off through the open door into the dark of the living room, beyond reach of the desk lamp's glow. What confronted him was the glum realization that this project could ultimately wrest from him his final gasp of breath on this earth.

In the gloom of his living room, he looked mortality in the face.

***

"Excuse me. Can I have a word with you?"

Edmund looked up from pruning the azalea bush in an outdoor display at Harbo's Garden Center. "Denise?"

She stood defiant, her auburn hair ratted back from her forehead. She wore black makeup, chunky skull jewelry on her neck and arms, and a black, sleeveless Ghost T-shirt. In her way, breathtaking.

"I took down the post," she said. "I suppose you've already made a copy of the image."

He wasn't sure whether to answer or not.

She glared at him. "I just want you to know that I'm nobody to mess with."

"You think I want to mess with you?"

"I'm saying that if you do, I'll hunt you down and leave you wishing you'd never seen me or that picture."

He set down the pruning shears and pulled off his work gloves. "I won't give you any trouble, Denise. You don't have to worry about me."

She eyed him skeptically. "Then what's your deal, Edmund?"

"I have no deal. I just recognized you from your picture on the website and said hi. That's all."

"How do I know you aren't some kind of weirdo?"

"I probably am some kind of weirdo. But not the dangerous kind."

Her shoulders dropped and she relaxed a little. "You won't try to get ahold of me?"

"Not if you don't want me to."

She studied his caramel features as if the fate of the nation rested on her appraisal. Then, surprisingly, she said, "What's your phone number?"

She wrote it down on the back of her hand. "If I feel like it, I'll give you a call. Maybe we have some things in common."

Just then, Taylin in her orange supervisor's vest sauntered up on them. She looked dismissively at Denise, then turned to Edmund. "How is that azalea bush coming?"

"Almost done, boss," he chirped.

She smiled. "I need you to fill in on register three, while Achmed takes his break."

"Okay. Be right there."

"Maybe I'll call you tonight, Edmund," Denise said. "Maybe I won't."

"Suit yourself," he replied pleasantly and followed Taylin to register three.

"Is that what you like?" Taylin asked when they were out of Denise's earshot.

"What do you mean?"

"You know, the Goth thing. Is that what you're into?"

"I'm into all sorts of stuff."

She was silent for a moment. Then she said, "Do you want to go out Wednesday night? We could get takeout from Noodles in Maple Grove and then walk over to Town Green Park. They have a free concert at the band shell that night. A Bee Gees tribute band. I hear they're pretty good."

Before he even had time to consider, he heard himself answer, "Sure."

But, already, his thoughts were carrying him elsewhere.

He wasn't sure what to make of Denise.

First, she threatened him. Then she seemed interested in him.

What kind of woman, really, would post a nude photo of herself splattered in blood and holding a whip made from a human spine, even if it was on the dark web? A seriously dangerous woman, perhaps. But, dangerous or not, there's no denying the allure of her in that aggressive pose.

It roused him on almost a genetic level, down in the nasty swamp of his primordial soup. He had to be careful when it came to her.

Also weighing on him was his obligation to the Bennetts. He was beginning to wonder if he had taken on too much. The end of summer was coming on fast, and he wanted to get as much work done on the garden as possible.

The previous weekend he'd managed to squeeze in enough daylight hours to spread the compost and set up the newly arrived arched, cherub trellis. The flagstones had also shown up, wrapped in plastic and stacked on a loading pallet. The delivery people had managed to back in their truck between the house and the garage without tearing up the patio or breaking anything.

Mrs. Bennett brought him glasses of cold water and engaged him encouragingly through the days, her birdlike flittings enthusiastic in the light of his progress.

This weekend he would lay the flagstones, seed the grass, and begin planting the flowers. He'd start with a creeping vine on the trellis, probably virgin's bower, and right up front he'd place clusters of aster blooms—Mrs. Bennett's favorite.

That night was a quiet one. Denise didn't call.

After a supper of curried potatoes and black bean soup, Edmund made popcorn, and he and Grandam watched a *Twilight Zone* marathon on one of her nostalgia channels. He told her about his workday, about his upcoming date with Taylin, about his concerns regarding the Bennetts' garden. She nodded. He didn't tell her about Denise. Denise was part of his other world, which Grandam must have known existed but had never shown an interest in exploring.

However, what failed to be a topic broached by Edmund and Grandam unfolded that night in a strange dream he had. In a surreal, black-and-white world, Denise, in the persona of an evil witch doctor from a headhunter tribe, stalked him through dense jungle. He

102

scrambled through marshy vines, cannibal epiphytes, lobster-claw flora, death's head orchids, through strangler figs, soapy carnauba palms, and stilt-rooted walking palms. He scratched and tore for his very life while she threatened him with ancient curses from craggy-toothed shadows just beyond his line of sight.

He awoke in the dead of night, bathed in sweat and sporting a painful erection.

What was he getting himself into?

That Wednesday, Taylin met him at Noodles and Company, once again donning her lip gloss, eye shadow, and orange-scented perfume. She wore a loose, satiny print blouse, mid-thigh shorts, and rope sandals. In his honor, he felt certain, she had painted her fingernails and toenails Goth black.

She held his hand as they walked to the band shell, carrying their to-go containers. Later, he put an arm around her shoulders as the cover band played "New York Mining Disaster 1941." *Don't talk too loud,* they warned, *you'll cause a landslide.* In context, a disturbing refrain. Taylin and he glanced at each other, and shared a kiss.

Despite his resistance, she was starting to grow on him.

Chapter Nineteen

Milo returned to his old haunts. Everything looked smaller than he remembered in the Milwaukee neighborhood he had fled more than 15 years ago: the houses, the alleyways, the weedy vacant lots. Some of the houses had been kept up, but many had not.

His old house was still there. It hadn't had a fresh coat of paint in all this time, and the gray grain of weathered wood siding showed through in spots. Iron now barred the basement windows, and a decal on the front door warned that the house was protected by an alarm system, though Milo suspected the system at this house consisted solely of the sticker. The front stoop had pulled away from the building and developed an ugly crack that went clean through to the ground. The yard was mostly dirt. The uneven sidewalk out front featured chalk hopscotch squares with crooked numbers, 1 through 10.

He considered knocking on the door and introducing himself as a former resident who just wanted to take a look around the old homestead, but decided that would just frighten the people inside. This was not a neighborhood that welcomed the approach of strangers.

He walked the blocks, the alleys and the footpaths, reliving pieces of his adolescence—the good and the bad—in flashes and blurs. Most of the storefronts had changed hands and reinvented themselves into something different. But Kayla's Table, a family-owned diner, was still in business so he went inside and ordered a grilled cheese sandwich, french fries, and a Coke.

"Nia?"

The smooth-featured Black waitress who brought him an amber glass of water studied his face. "Do I know you?"

"I'm a ghost from your past. Long time ago. I used to hang out with your brother Jerome. I'm Milo Castellanos." It felt strange, saying his real name out loud.

"Sure. I remember." She set down the glass, wiped her wet fingers on her apron, and shook Milo's hand.

Nia, it turned out, was a walking repository of neighborhood lore.

His daddy, he learned, was doing time in Waupun Correctional Institute, a maximum-security penitentiary in Waupun, Wisconsin, for having shaken to death Milo's baby brother, Truman. Milo felt sad about this, but the truth was he barely remembered Truman, or any of his other siblings, for that matter. They were just sort of place-keepers in the chronology of his life.

His mousy mother, her remaining five charges in tow, had traveled out East somewhere, as far from imprisoned Stash as her little feet would carry her. Some thought New York. Some thought Massachusetts. He seemed to recall she had a relative in Boston. Either way, he would let her be. She had been through enough tragedy in her life without him visiting his horror show on her.

Jerome, Nia told him, was an architect at Broadstone Design in Dallas. Her other brother, Malik, was a foreman at the Leinenkugel Brewing Company in Chippewa Falls.

"What do you do?" she asked him.

"I'm a union carpenter in Schaumburg, Illinois."

She left him to take the order of an Asian family at the next table. When his sandwich came, Milo ate in silence, staring through the diner's dusty front window. He decided he had already seen enough of Milwaukee for one lifetime.

Milo had spent nearly two weeks living in Hank Kowarski's condominium, enjoying juicy cuts of Hank with mushrooms, rice, and whatever fresh or frozen vegetables were on hand. He'd had Hank stir fried, roasted, and boiled.

He'd lugged Hank to the bathtub and butchered him there. The hands, feet, and head were removed first, double-bagged and, in the early morning when the halls were empty, dumped down the garbage shoot near the elevator. Then he cut away his favorite steaks. Some of the flanks he froze, some he refrigerated.

He'd read that when the Uruguay turboprop carrying an amateur rugby team and their families crashed, leaving them stranded for 71 days in the Andes Mountains, they'd had to survive by eating the corpses of those killed in the crash. Eventually the survivors were forced to eat rotten flesh. They found this to be harmless and said it tasted like cheese. Milo had tried this himself years ago but it didn't appeal to his palate. If he couldn't have his flesh fresh off the hoof, he insisted it be well-preserved.

He would have stayed longer at the condominium if Hank's cell phone hadn't begun ringing incessantly. Most of the calls came from Hank's workplace, but others were beginning to show up more frequently. From Mom and Dad, and from someone named Prudence who Milo guessed was also one of Hank's relatives. Eventually, someone would call the landlord or the police, and Milo didn't want to be found in a missing man's condo.

Hank Kowarski would never be immortalized as one of the Midwest Butcher's victims. Once Milo had thoroughly dissected Hank and cleaned the home of all trace evidence, the carpenter would simply become one of the thousands of Americans who go permanently missing every year. For Milo, this was a forensic countermeasure to help keep law enforcement from nipping too close to his heels. More than half of Milo's kills had been assigned to the rolls of the mysteriously vanished.

The loss of this credit wouldn't have bothered him even if he had considered it. In many ways, the Butcher was just a role he played for his enjoyment and the entertainment of the masses. His true purpose was more fluid, morphing from one grand ethereal perception to another, each interchangeable and transformative in its way. Among his many layers, the legacy of the Midwest Butcher pulsed in and out of importance. The only constants for him were the urge to roam the corridors of the Midwest and to serve the needs of his demon queen, Baba Yaga.

In one of those coincidences that Milo preferred to think of as destiny, he had found something in Hank's condo that pointed him to the next leg of his quest. On a bedside bookshelf, among Louis L'Amour and Max Brand westerns, rested a surprisingly incongruous, almost scholarly tome from the University of Minnesota Press. A translation of folk stories called *Russian Wonder Tales of Baba Yaga* by Yegor Dzhurmongaliev.

What a find! The book felt electric in his hands as he thumbed through the contents.

The back of the book pictured the author, a stern-faced old-timer with a corona of wispy white hair and a green glass eye. "Yegor Dzhurmongaliev," the bio read, "is an award-winning author and translator who has produced more than 30 books on subjects of Russian folklore, history, and literary criticism. He holds a post-graduate degree in Slavic languages from Columbia University and is a contributing editor of *Studia Slavica et Balcanica Petropolitana*. He enjoys cooking, classical music, and computer chess. Yegor, known as George to his friends, lives on the shore of scenic Lake Minnetonka, the largest lake in the Twin Cities metropolitan area."

Milo had already feasted on the book twice, and it left him with a wealth of new information and dozens of new questions about his dark mistress. At last, the stars had aligned to offer him a path to someone who was a bona fide expert on his cherished entity.

After leaving Kayla's Table, Milo hopped an Uber to the Greyhound station on West St. Paul Avenue and bought a $44 outbound economy ticket. According to the schedule, he would arrive in Minneapolis at 11:15 p.m.

***

Somehow Rudy had gotten on the subject of the JFK assassination, an event he surprisingly did not blame on the Illuminati.

"What people don't realize was that Joe Kennedy, the president's father, was a member of that society, so there is no way they were behind it. According to Oswald's mother, Marguerite, the real story is that Kennedy and Texas Governor John Connelly, who rode together in an open car, got into a heated political argument and shot each other."

Edmund knew better than to comment on Rudy's ramblings, but this theory severely strained credibility. "The president of the United States and the governor of Texas shot each other in an open limousine during a public parade? Wouldn't someone have noticed that?"

"Some people did. Those people died mysterious deaths. Plant a few false flags and doctor an eight-millimeter film, and you can change the course of recorded history, Edmund."

"Hmmm." *You really can't win with conspiracy nuts.* He looked out the side window, wondering whether his driver even believed the world was round.

The Cadillac purred up the smooth expanse of the Bennetts' driveway and into the garage. As Edmund climbed out, he noticed a slow-moving, devil-red sports car creeping along on the street below. He caught Denise's profile behind the steering wheel. When their eyes met, she sped up and drove off.

Did Denise live around here? Maybe she was visiting someone. She couldn't possibly have been following him, could she?

He wondered about that as he unpacked hostas and ferns from the Caddy's trunk.

The day was overcast, and he'd worked that morning at Harbo's outdoor sales floor with one eye on the sky. So far, the weather had cooperated remarkably well with his gardening agenda. But now, under the threat of rain, he needed to make the most of his time. He carried the planters to the backyard where the asters and chrysanthemums were already taking root around the trellis arch, and seedlings of turf were popping up green all around. As he made his examinations, he plucked weeds by hand wherever they cropped up.

He decided to leave the ferns in their containers, to acclimate to conditions for a day before repotting them. But the hardy and more shade-tolerant hostas needed to be in the ground today if he had any hope of sticking to his schedule.

He gathered tools from the gardener's cottage and went to work.

With hostas, the darker the color, the more shade-tolerant the plants. Edmund had individually selected these plants for their dark foliage and the absence of any signs of crown or leaf rot. He dug the holes for them about a foot deep and spaced widely enough to eventually accommodate fully mature plants.

Edmund stripped the plastic from the pallet of flagstones. He rolled out and laid the first three stones, which wound through the arched trellis. Then he carefully counted out the remaining flagstones, divided their width by the distance between the patio and the cottage, and marked orange circles with spray-paint where he thought the others should be laid, pending final approval from the Bennetts. The general pattern of the stones was agreed upon, but the distance between the stones was still up in the air. If additional stones were needed, he would buy them singly from Harbo's.

The clouds spit random raindrops at him, but he soldiered through and was pleased with his progress. Tomorrow was Sunday, his day off from Harbo's. He would lay more of the stone path, partially line it with ferns, deciduous azalea shrubs and more asters. In his mind, he could see the garden blooming up on all sides in a joyous blending of hues.

Working on the garden soothed him, gave him some relief from his conflicted thoughts about Denise and Taylin.

He was absorbed in this sense of calm when Mr. Bennett walked up with his neighbor George and introduced them to each other.

"Edmund, this is George Dzhurmongaliev, who I was telling you about. The Russian translator and writer. He's interested in having you take a peek at his flower garden, when you get a chance."

George, closer to Rudy's age than Mr. Bennett's, shook Edmund's hand. The writer looked disheveled and in desperate need of a nap. Like Mr. Bennett, he wore the tan Bermuda shorts, polo shirt and wide-brimmed straw hat that was something of a uniform on the lake. George's legs were pale and veined, unlike Mr. Bennett's, which had more coloring.

"Elon here has been bragging you up to me, Edmund. He's very complimentary of your talents as a gardener."

"Mr. Bennett is too kind. What sort of books do you write, George?"

"Mostly English translations of Russian folktales. I'm working on a volume that traces back the origins of a legendary folk character to her pagan roots. It's based on some fairly esoteric writings and, hopefully, will be groundbreaking."

"Sounds interesting."

"It is quite fascinating, but more taxing than anything I've ever written before." There was a glint of something awful in the way George said this. "Anyway, feel free to drop by my place if you get a chance. My garden could benefit from your advice, I'm sure."

"Well, we'll let you get back to your work, Edmund," Mr. Bennett said, leading George away toward the patio and the house. The neighbors launched into a dour exchange on the subject of Minnetonka property taxes as their voices faded.

Edmund finished up an hour or so before nightfall when the intermittent raindrops broke into a steady drizzle. Mrs. Bennett invited him to supper that evening, but he politely declined. Instead, he would have a late dinner with Grandam and then meet up later with Taylin.

Customarily, a third date between consenting adults can come with certain carnal expectations, but nothing of the sort took place with Taylin that night. She picked him up in the rain in her white sedan, and they drove to a tavern in Northeast Minneapolis called Lucky Penny's, where it was trivia night. They drank beers, ate french fries, and guessed at trivia questions. Taylin won $10 at pull-tabs.

It was almost closing time when they walked from the watering hole, hand in hand, smiling, and stopped under awnings to kiss several times. As Taylin unlocked the passenger-side door for him, she asked, a little starry-eyed, "We're having fun together, aren't we, Eddie?"

"Yes." And it was true.

Chapter Twenty

From CannibalAnimal24 in Bear Dance, Montana, a statistician: "I imagine myself like a suckling pig, my flesh rubbed with kosher salt, roasting on a spit that you've shoved in through my mouth and out my rectum. Steel prongs at either end hold me in place. You rotate me over the hot coals, the curls of my head, eyebrows, lashes, chest, armpits, and groin singe away to ash, surrendering wisps of gossamer smoke. Slowly I take on a burnished color, and the fat beneath my hide begins to melt and boil. My eyes wither in the sockets. The intense heat raises blisters on my skin that become crispy pustules that slowly crack open. Perhaps you'll braise me with curried ketchup or a brandied fig sauce. When at last I am ready, you can remove the spit and slice me into juicy, steamy cutlets. What a feast you will enjoy. *Bon appétit*, my lover."

***

As he neared Minneapolis that rainy evening, Milo took a break from his Baba Yaga book. He'd read through it three and a half times since first liberating it from Hank Kowarski's bedside bookshelf, and the details of it were burning into his brain like an acid-etched engraving.

The book revealed Baba Yaga as others had known her before. She of the long, bloated nose, of the drooping breasts, the gleaming eyes, the snapping iron teeth, maniacal and vicious, soaring on a whirlwind of death and destruction through the lives of those who challenged her. But it was also Baba Yaga as imagined by the author Yegor Dzhurmongaliev: Baba Yaga as an actual clawing, visceral force of nature that howled in the hollows of humanity's bones. Who cast a spell of darkness across the sky like an eclipse of the sun. Who shook mountains to dust and ran like glowing lava from cracks in the Earth. A goddess of ruin that Milo had thought only himself capable of glimpsing.

He smiled. Someone else knew and understood. Yegor Dzhurmongaliev, resident of Minnetonka, Minnesota, holder, for the moment, of the reins of Milo's destiny.

City lights approached the bus from the distance, and he let his mind drift.

In the seat next to him, riding the aisle, a thin, tallow-complexioned young man with collar-length hair snoozed fitfully, his face shapeless in the dark. Sprinkled among the empty seats all around, passengers slept, read, played with their phones. To a person, each was clueless that the Midwest Butcher nestled snuggly in their midst.

Milo mused on a peculiar Canadian named Vince Weiguang Li, who'd once boarded a Greyhound bus like this one at a station in Erickson, Manitoba. The other passengers on that bus had also been clueless. But not for long.

Shortly after midnight in July of 2008, their naivety was forever shattered when Vince, all at once, lost his ever-loving mind and erupted in a grisly, murderous outburst.

Vince, a sturdily built immigrant from Dandong, China, had a lot to feel down about. Life in his adopted country had fallen far short of expectations. First, he was unable to find employment in his chosen profession of software engineer. Instead, necessity forced him to work at unfulfilling, menial jobs. Compounding matters, his wife divorced him in 2006. And, somewhere along the way, in 2003, he was hospitalized after being found wandering a random Ontario highway, following the sun as he claimed God instructed him to do. According to his ex-wife, Vince often talked to himself and would periodically disappear for days on end.

On this day, a forty-year-old Vince was traveling to Winnipeg for a job interview, when another passenger, Tim McLean, a winsome twenty-two-year-old carnival worker sitting toward the rear of the bus, caught his eye.

Why Tim McLean? Who knows? Maybe he emitted the same lonely-boy aura that Milo found so appealing. Maybe there was no discernible reason for selecting this man, just a feeling that it was Tim's time to die.

Most of the passengers were asleep in their seats when the screaming began.

Startled awake, they turned to the source of the wailing, and saw Vince, again and again, plunging a knife into Tim's neck and chest. Blood sputtered and splashed in angry gouts with each swing of the blade. In the confined space, pandemonium broke out, with Tim struggling vainly to get away from the madman, and the panicked passengers bolting for the exits.

The driver stopped the bus and radioed the Royal Canadian Mounted Police in nearby Portage la Prairie, then joined his rattled passengers on the roadside. He and a few brave souls briefly ventured back into the bus, hoping to talk down Vince, but by then, the madman was storming up and down the aisle, gripping McLean's now-severed head by the hair.

Adding to the horrified passengers' trauma, Vince began cutting off chunks of his victim's skin and greedily wolfing them down.

Canadian police tried to talk Vince into surrendering, but the crazed killer just kept slicing and devouring bloody clumps of flesh. He carved off and placed some of the body parts in plastic bags, which he squirreled throughout the bus. Finally, at about 1:30 a.m., the standoff ended.

Giving himself up, Vince begged the cops to kill him, but instead they took him into custody. In his pockets, they discovered Tim McLean's nose, ears, and tongue.

Surprisingly, after being confined for just eight years at the Selkirk Mental Health Center, Vince regained his freedom and melted into anonymity. Milo often wondered whether Vince had ever considered resuming his wicked ways.

The bus station in Minneapolis was downtown, across the street from First Avenue, the nightclub where Prince filmed segments of *Purple Rain*. Milo's fellow Greyhound passengers scattered across the drenched pavement into the drizzling night. With collars turned up, they hunched like modern-day Quasimodos.

Milo, carrying his canvas tote bag, trudged down a backstreet and was swallowed by shadows.

Chapter Twenty-One

T he next morning, Edmund awoke to the ringing of his cell
phone. The display read UNKNOWN CALLER. "Hello?"
"It's me, Edmund. Denise Nils."
"Okay."

"I wanted to explain why I followed you yesterday. I didn't want
you to think I was stalking you."

"Uh-hmmm." He sat up in bed and stretched his legs.

"It's just that I never expected to meet in person anyone who had
seen that post. And now that it's happened, I'm not sure how I feel
about it. You understand?"

"Not exactly."

"Can we meet for lunch?"

"I have gardening work today. At the house in Minnetonka, where
you saw me."

"Well, you must take a lunch break. Why don't I drive by and pick
you up? Say, noonish."

"Alright."

"See you then." She hung up.

He couldn't have asked for a better day to work in the garden,
sunny and not too hot. He asked Rudy to swing by Harbo's, and they
loaded up the Cadillac's trunk with hostas and begonias. On the way
to Minnetonka, Rudy explained how members of England's Royal

Family could, in reality, be shape-shifting lizards, but all Edmund could think about was Denise's phone call.

It was just past nine when the Caddy arrived at the Bennetts' house. Milo went immediately to work, placing planters, weeding, spreading fresh grass seed, rolling out more flagstones, planting ferns and the additional hostas and begonias in rowed groupings. He had worked three hours straight when Mrs. Bennett cleared her throat behind him.

"Edmund, there's a young lady here to see you." Mrs. Bennett raised an eyebrow. "She *says* she's a friend of yours."

In a low-cut, sleeveless tee, and a black-and-white striped skirt, Denise stood to one side, black-painted fingernails gripping one cocked hip. Her eye makeup mimicked Alice Cooper's, and she'd braided her reddish-brown hair in Wednesday Addams pigtails. She wore one earring, a shirtless male figure with axes in his outstretched hands, which Edmund recognized as a Santería charm.

"Yes, it's okay, Mrs. Bennett."

She smiled and nodded, then plodded off to the house.

"Looks like you have quite a project on your hands," Denise said.

"Yeah, well, I have a ways to go."

They rode into town, stereo blasting Megadeth's "Countdown to Extinction." No surprise that Denise was into thrash metal. On the second track, the singer decried robotic leaders with corroded brains who made people dance like marionettes.

The song lyrics reminded him of something he had read in a translation of the Buddha. "Believe nothing," the enlightened one said, "no matter where you read it or who said it, no matter if I have said it, unless it agrees with your own reason and your own common sense."

He guessed that was the gist of what Megadeth was getting at.

They pulled up at a place called Maggie's Restaurant. After perusing the menu, they decided to split a cheese pizza.

"I'm sorry if I upset you, Denise. I was as surprised as you were when I recognized you at Pamela's funeral."

"What made you look up that website?"

"Curiosity, I guess. My grandam says we're descended from the Marind Anims of New Guinea."

A look of amazement swept her features. "The Cannibal Gardeners?"

"You've heard of us?"

Against her black lipstick, her teeth showed extremely white. "The Cannibal Gardeners were prehistoric head-hunters. Joseph Campbell wrote about them. To appease their gods, they held this ceremony that collapsed time. They chanted, pounded on drums made of logs, and blew into some kind of instruments that made this incredible noise they believed to be the voices of their gods calling back to them from the beginning of time.

"The ceremony went on for days, as I recall, and culminated in a vast orgy that they believed united them into a single spirit."

"Yes. I've heard about all that. Grandam is quite the historian."

"Did she tell you that, at the end of the ceremony, a naked boy and a girl, painted and oiled, and dressed in symbolic amulets, were selected to couple on a platform with heavy logs suspended over them? As they embraced in coital ecstasy, someone tugged loose a rope, and the logs came crashing down on them, killing them. Then the tribe dragged their bodies from beneath the logs, cut them up, roasted, and ate them."

Edmund glanced up at her. Her eyes were bright with excitement.

"She may have told me something like that. My ancestors were often given to extremes. Why do you think they did that?"

Denise shrugged, a purple bra strap sliding down one shoulder. "It has to do with their mythology, which was modeled on the life and death of plants. What I think is, they went to great lengths to build up this shared sense of unity, of otherworldly timelessness, and then brought it all crashing down. Heartlessly, amid lovemaking, as part of a realization that Mother Nature can be a wicked bitch. My guess is you had to be a part of the ceremony to understand it fully."

Their voices took on a measured quality as they tread lightly on more personal matters.

"Sometimes, on the dark web, I look at pictures," Edmund said. "Of people twisted in death, on highways and battlefields, in the wake of earthquakes and massacres and executions. Do you think that's because of who my ancestors were?"

"Maybe. Do the images arouse you?"

"No. Not usually. It's not like that. It's more like I'm curious to read the expressions in their faces and their eyes. I'm looking for something, but I'm not quite sure what it is."

"Did my picture arouse you?"

Edmund winced slightly. "Of course."

"Was it my nakedness, or was it the blood and the skull and the blasphemous symbols?"

He considered the question before answering. "It was all of it, I guess."

"You're Raoul153, aren't you?"

Now it was Edmund's turn to feel exposed.

"How did you know?"

"Some detective work. A little black juju." She smiled mysteriously. "I've read through all your past posts. Lately, you've been calling for volunteers to be eaten by you. Is that something you're really interested in?" Her eyes widened.

"Well, I read about this German guy who ran an ad like that on a website, and he got several replies."

"Armind Meiwes. His mother was said to have sold her soul to Satan."

"Well, you know the story then."

"Did your mother sell her soul to Satan?"

"I'm not sure whether or not my mother believed in Satan. She and my father died in a car crash when I was young."

The waitress came with their pizza, and they each pulled off a slice.

Denise took a bite, chewed, and continued, talking around a mouthful. "Armind Meiwes advertised online for a 'young, well-built man who wants to be eaten.'"

"You seem quite informed on the history of cannibalism."

"I read a lot." She grinned at him, a speck of tomato sauce on her chin. "Anyway, as I recall, Meiwes received over two hundred replies, including one from a forty-three-year-old computer engineer named Bernd Brandes. They exchanged emails and ultimately met in ... Berlin, was it? No, Brandes was from Berlin. They met at Meiwes' house in Rotenberg, a rundown old mansion where Meiwes lived alone. They say he sometimes walked around the house wearing the clothes of his dead mother. Shades of *Psycho*, right?"

She swallowed, took another bite, chewed, and swallowed again.

"He had this room," she said, "that he specially prepared in the attic of his house, where he planned to bring Brandes. The room, which had no windows, was painted red and black and had meat hooks hanging from the ceiling and, in the middle of the room, a butcher's table long enough to accommodate a full-size adult. He also had a wire cage up there. Police described it as being something out of a horror film. Meiwes called it his slaughterhouse."

Edmund looked down at the melted cheese and tomato sauce of the half-eaten pizza slice on his plate.

"Nearly all the people who had responded to Meiwes ad were goofs," Denise said. "Freaks who were just feeding their fantasies about being eaten, but not intending to go all in. Brandes, however, was dead serious. Before he left for Rotenberg, he drew up his will."

Denise recounted how, on March 9, 2001, in a chilling scene captured on a camcorder, Meiwes, using a butcher knife, sliced off Brandes' penis. After sautéing it in butter and garlic, the two of them devoured it. Then Meiwes hauled Brandes, much weakened from blood loss, to a bathtub and left him in warm water to bleed out. Ten hours later, Brandes was still alive, so Meiwes fetched the butcher knife and, while kissing Brandes softly of the lips, drove the blade into Brandes' throat.

Meiwes dismembered Brandes, and cut off about 65 pounds of meat, which he refrigerated or froze. The remnants of the corpse were buried in the backyard, not far from the grill Meiwes would use to fry up some of these human steaks.

"Meiwes claimed that when he ate Brandes," Denise said, "he felt the man's presence come alive within. Become part of him. His memories of Brandes became clearer, and he felt he developed some of Brandes' traits. For instance, he became more adept at speaking English, a language at which Brandes was fluent."

Even though Brandes was filmed being complicit in his own death, and there was no crime of cannibalism on the books in Germany at the time, Meiwes was eventually convicted of second-degree murder and sentenced to life in prison.

"Do you believe that when you eat people you absorb their essence, Denise?"

She licked sauce from her fingers. "That's one reason used to justify the practice. Some ancient tribes even ate their kin out of respect, believing the spirits of dead would live on within them."

"What do you believe?"

"I believe being eaten beats being buried in the ground. If I die before you do, you have my permission to eat me."

At this, he felt a warm flow of blood enter his lower belly.

"Are you someone I should be afraid of?" Denise said unexpectedly, studying him.

"I was about to ask you the same thing."

She chuckled. "I like you, Edmund. You're cordial but a little twisted. Our interests overlap in common areas. I think we can be friends."

"Agreed."

She gave him her phone number, which he entered into his contacts.

They finished their meal in silence. Then Edmund said, "I should be getting back to the Bennetts'."

On the drive back, Edmund was treated to the first few songs from the album *We Are Not Your Kind* by Slipknot. At one point the singer, under rapid-fire guitar chords, sang of how he'd never kill himself to save his soul. Was that nihilist angst or a rejection of martyrdom? Or maybe just a renunciation of suicide.

He wondered what the Buddha would have thought about that. "The root of all suffering is attachment," the Buddha said, but what of our attachment to life itself? What if the suffering of living comes to outweigh all other concerns?

Is that why Brandes allowed himself to be eaten?

When they pulled into the driveway, Mr. Bennett stood on the front lawn, talking with George.

Edmund opened the door and was about to exit, when Denise said, "Who's that man?"

"Mr. Bennett?"

"Which one is he?"

"He's the one in the white shorts. The younger of the two."

"Who's he's talking to? The one in the fuzzy slippers. I've seen that man's picture somewhere before."

"That's George. The next-door neighbor. Actually, his name is Yegor something-or-other. Don't ask me to pronounce his last name. Something Russian."

"Yegor Dzhurmongaliev?"

Edmund froze. "Yes. That sounds right. Do you know him?"

"The writer?"

"Yes."

Denise turned off her engine. "I've got to meet him. He's brilliant."

They strolled over to the two men, Denise leading the way.

The old-timers paused in their conversation and looked at her as if they weren't sure what they were looking at. In all fairness, Denise's appearance was more than a little unconventional.

"Mr. Dzhurmongaliev? Yegor Dzhurmongaliev?"

"Yes, that's me," George said, losing his stunned demeanor. "Kudos on the pronunciation, by the way. Do I know you?"

Mr. Bennett still looked as if he expected to be attacked with a machete at any moment.

"No," she said, "but I've read several of your books and recognized you from your pictures on the book jackets. I just wanted to say, I think you're brilliant."

George blushed, and shook Denise's hand. Mr. Bennett markedly relaxed.

"Thank you, young lady," George said. "We scholars aren't used to experiencing much in the way of fandom."

"Well, you've got a fan in me," she said. "My name is Denise Nils, and I don't want to interrupt you, but perhaps we could meet sometime and discuss Russian folklore. I'd be especially interested in your thoughts on Baba Yaga."

At the mention of the demon witch's name, George's face went slack. Nonetheless, he agreed. "How can I say no to a true fan? If you come by tomorrow, no, Tuesday night I could fix you dinner. Nothing fancy, but I make a mean borscht. You could bring Edmund along, too, and he can perhaps offer some advice on my beleaguered garden."

"I can come Tuesday," Edmund said, "but I'm vegetarian."

Denise looked at Edmund as if he'd just confessed to killing a Boy Scout.

"I can make it meatless," George said. "That's no problem."

"Tuesday it is," Denise said. She and George shook hands, then Edmund walked her back to her car. Before getting in, she gave him a hard look. "Vegetarian? Really?"

Chapter Twenty-Two

T hat night, Edmund was more confused than ever. Taylin versus Denise: a contest he wasn't even sure genuinely existed. After all, Denise had never indicated an interest in him other than friendship. Nonetheless, she mesmerized him.

When he thought about Taylin, he felt a warmth that tugged at him. She genuinely cared for him; he was sure of that. She probably had for some time. He could see in her the potential for contentment, possibly even happiness. And they got along surprisingly well.

Denise, on the other hand, if he could even convince her to take him on as a lover, would quickly tire of him. Use him up and spit him out, probably heartbroken and mentally mangled. Still, as a conversationalist, she was delightful. She had a way of lighting a fire in him that no one had quite managed before.

"Grandam, I had lunch with a woman today who knew about the Cannibal Gardeners."

"When you told her those were your ancestors, did she run for the hills?"

"No. Not Denise. I think she was more shocked to learn I was a vegetarian."

Grandam chuckled softly. "We are all walking contradictions, Edmund. That's just called existing as a human being."

"There's something about her that's exciting. I know she's trouble, but common sense doesn't seem to be in the driver's seat when it comes to how I feel about her."

"How do you feel about the other one?"

He sighed. "Being with Taylin is ... comfortable. I'd say I feel content with her. She's dependable and loyal."

"She's the one who calls you Eddie?"

"Yes," he said sheepishly. "Well. I'm getting used to that."

Grandam rocked in her rocking chair. "I don't want to tell you how to conduct your love life, Edmund, but there's more to love than lust. Ideally, there's a partnership, friendship, companionship. You need a helper, someone to support you, someone you can rely on. That's what I think, but I've never met these women of yours, so all I have to go on is what you tell me."

That's where they left it. Edmund went online. Grandam watched *The Man from U.N.C.L.E.* on her nostalgia channel.

He kept off the dark web, instead browsing listlessly through emails, news sites, gardening blogs. He knew he should phone Taylin or Denise, but he needed a break from all that. He went to a gaming site and played *Civilization III*, an old-school strategy game. (In Edmund's opinion, they ruined the game with *IV*.) He lost himself in building cities and armies, in battles and diplomacy. When he looked up from the screen, it was after eleven. Grandam was snoozing in her chair, illuminated by the black-and-white flicker of *Combat!* He had work tomorrow and he really should go to bed, but he was enjoying himself. *One more campaign*, he thought.

When he finally turned in, it was nearly two o'clock in the morning.

***

Parts of Hennepin Avenue can get sketchy after dark, but that night Milo walked the grimmest sections of that Minneapolis street with ease, protected by the presence within him, his iron-jawed mistress who flitted now and then in the periphery of his vision.

Carrying her with all her parts was often a burden, and tonight was no exception, but she gave him the courage to walk past restless groupings of young men of all ethnicities, past eyes that studied him from the mouths of alleys and the shadows of doorways.

"What'cha got in the bag, friendo?" someone called, but he just moved on, impervious to their taunts.

He had spent the previous night in a homeless shelter, his wallet stuffed down the front of his jeans, his canvas tote bag hugged to his chest beneath a cotton throw. He had slept on a cot, off and on, in a roomful of cots filled with fellow sleepers. The old and the luckless, the cunning and the insane, their breath and their whispers orbited him in the dark like a halo of gnats. He slept in spells just long enough to dream, and every dream was about her clawing out from the cavern of his throat, emerging in a blinding fury accompanied by thunderclaps and spiked crags of lightning. Her worshipers bowed to the ground in stone enclaves; some burned to ash by the heat of her wrath. These dreams were signs of her growing impatience.

He remembered where the boarding house was, but he couldn't remember the last time he'd been there.

When he ran from Milwaukee years ago, he lost his sense of linear time. In his memory, events slid back and forth, rearranging themselves in a chronology of their choosing. Maybe it was Baba Yaga who stole this perception from him. According to the Dzhurmongaliev book in his canvas tote, one of the demon's powers was mastery over the flow of time. If this was true, it explained a lot.

For instance, he knew he had met the ancient Russian vagrant at a hobo jungle outside Houghton, Michigan, either shortly before or after being inspired by the Dahmer documentary to eat the old girl in St. Paul. The Russian had first introduced him to Baba Yaga, so the Russian must have come afterward. *Right?*

The harder he thought about it, the more confused he became. But the details of that fateful meeting were clear as a noonday sun.

The young Milo happened upon the gathered men early one evening in a wooded clearing not far from the rail yards. These men were hobos as Milo always imagined hobos to be: rough characters, poorly spoken, dressed in rags, filthy, unshaven, and wary. As he broke the circle of their campfire's light, the gaunt, greasy faces all turned his way, eyes slit and glaring.

"Whadda ya want?" a voice growled from the dark.

Some of the figures rose, some just coiled to crouches as if preparing to spring.

"I don't want anything," Milo said. "I just arrived by boxcar, and I'm passing through."

"If you know what's good for you, you'll just keep passing." The fellow who said this was shirtless and dressed in a kilt, of all things. His chest loomed massive, matted with gray hair, and grimy. His face appeared sort of squished together in a way that reminded Milo of a cartoon character.

"I'm going, I'm going," Milo said.

"Not so fast," one of the crouchers barked. Standing up on impossibly thin legs in a dingy suit that in better days perhaps had clothed an undertaker, a hatchet-faced derelict took a step toward Milo. "You don't have any money on you, do you?"

"Not a nickel." This was a lie. He had several dollars hidden in his sock. At the time, he wasn't sure where the money came from. Sometimes it just appeared.

"Make him turn out his pockets," someone said.

Hatchet Face stepped toward him, menacing. "Let's see what you got!"

"Yeah!" shouted the man in the kilt.

Milo started to pull out his pockets for their inspection when several of the hobos rushed him and grabbed him by the arms.

"Let's see what you've got," Hatchet Face repeated.

Their filthy hands rifled through his pockets. They ripped open his shirt, sending buttons flying. The zipper of his pants riffled open and the coarse jean fabric dropped to his ankles. The next thing he knew he was naked, and they were dividing up the money from his sock and laughing at him. Rough hands slammed him to the grass.

When he came to, someone was squirming on his back, flopping and yowling. Milo's bowels felt as if they were filled with crushed glass.

They didn't all have a go at him—maybe five or six did—then they let him be, and he stumbled around searching for his clothes.

He was shivering, in a daze, when the old Russian brought him to the fireside where the heat of the flames warmed the boy. "You stay to me," the Russian said in bad English. "I watch out for you."

Milo felt the urge to scurry off and get lost in the night, but when the Russian draped a woolen blanket over Milo's shoulders and gripped him in big bear hug, the boy melted. Hypnotized by the flicker of the fire and the drone of the old Russian's broken English, Milo was suddenly too tired to rise, too tired to flee.

The Russian talked first about the streets of his neighborhood in St. Petersburg when he was a child. The shabby storefronts and overcrowded tenements. The unbending heat in summer. How he had roamed through the dust and stench like a feral cat. Witnessing clumsy sots staggering from pothouses, faded whores on every corner, soldiers striking people down for simply getting in their way. He told of going days without eating, and how he sometimes lied to himself that he had only been one day without food when really he had been two or more.

To help him get his mind off the hunger, his mother sometimes told him tales of Baba Yaga, a mysterious witch who lived in a house that turned around and around on chicken legs. A fence of human bones penned the house in to keep it from wandering off. It was not a place that anyone would choose to visit, and many who entered it were never seen again.

The Russian remembered one of the tales was about Vasilisa the Beautiful who was the daughter of a merchant. When she was eight years old, her mother died. On her deathbed, her mother gave her a wooden doll, which she told Vasilisa to never show to anyone. This doll, her mother told her, was enchanted. Whenever Vasilisa encountered difficulties in life, if she gave the doll a pinch of food and a drop of water, it would find a way to help her. These were the last words her mother spoke to her.

Eventually, Vasilisa's father remarried a woman who already had two daughters of her own. The woman and her daughters were cold to Vasilisa, treating her like a servant in her father's house. One day her father left the village on business, and his wife sold the house and moved Vasilisa and her stepsisters to a dreary old house far away in the country, next to a thick forest.

Late one evening, they ran out of fire and Vasilisa's stepmother sent Vasilisa off into the woods to borrow a flame from the nearest neighbor who lived far down a path. That neighbor turned out to be none other than the evil Baba Yaga.

Vasilisa walked through the scary woods in the dead of night, comforted only by her wooden doll, and, as day broke, a Cossack in white suddenly appeared. The rider's skin and hair were purest white, as were his clothes, horse, saddle, and tack. It was as if the rider and his horse had plunged into white paint.

Fear seized her, stopping her in her tracks. Who could this Cossack be but a ghost that prowled the woods at night?

After regarding her curiously, the rider reared on his steed and charged off into the forest.

As the day stretched to noon, Vasilisa continued to follow the trail, wondering if she would ever come to a house.

Still not wholly calmed from her confrontation with the white rider, her path was once again crossed by a Cossack, this one dressed all in red, carrying a fiery torch. The rider's skin was red as a ruby, as were his hair, his horse and all his horse's gear. He paused to consider her as if preparing to climb down from his steed and attack. But instead, he also reared his horse and disappeared into the woods.

Vasilisa, still having seen no houses, thought perhaps she should head back. She hadn't eaten since the previous night, and lightheadedness threatened to topple her with every step. But she pressed on.

As night began to fall, she once more encountered a Cossack on horseback. This one was all black, blacker than any man she had ever seen, black as an abyss, dressed in black on a black horse with all black gear. A perfect herald for the approaching darkness of night. This one scowled at her, black-gloved hands gripping the reins as if possessed of a mighty urge to wrap them around her neck. But, in the end, he too headed for the surrounding trees.

As he rode past, fear so swept Vasilisa that she nearly fainted. However, just ahead in a glade, she saw that she had come at last upon a house, the most curious house she had ever seen.

The dwelling rotated slowly on what appeared to be chicken legs. Around the house was a fence with posts made from human bones. Atop the posts were skulls, though one post was in want of a skull. As she neared the place, the skulls' empty eye sockets took on a vermilion glow, as if alerted to her presence. Soon the entire clearing glowed with the eerie light.

Under their watchful gaze, she could not take a single step closer.

That was where Baba Yaga found her hours later when the witch swooped in on her flying mortar....

The old Russian's tale was still playing through in Milo's head when he came to the dull-cerise brick boarding house with the rusted iron gate just off Hennepin Avenue, where Cassandra lived. He opened the gate and trod the cracked walkway to the drooping steps and up them. The last time he was here, the doorbell hadn't worked, and he'd had to pound on the door until someone opened it. He decided to try the bell anyway, and this time it worked. He pressed it, waited, pressed it again. The doorknob twisted, and an African American woman in a robe stood in the narrow gap allowed by the door's chain. She eyed him suspiciously.

"Who are you?" the woman demanded. Milo could tell from her stance that she had one foot braced behind the door.

"Milo Castellanos. I'm a friend of Cassandra. Is she in?"

"Cassandra!" the woman called out, loud enough to startle Milo. "Someone to see you. Says he's a friend. Milo something-or-other."

From the ill-lit living room over the watchwoman's shoulder, came movement. *Yes, it was her.* Cassandra, in worn, silky pajamas, stepped to the door, closed it to disengage the chain, and opened it fully. Milo worked to tamp down his excitement, though for him excitement was more akin to a mild cheerfulness.

Cassandra stood in the glow of the streetlights, her librarian eyeglasses dangling from a cord around her neck. She was fortyish, with Jamaican coloring, a long, flat nose, and alert somewhat protruding brown eyes. "Milo," she said, baring her brilliant ivories in a smile. "How are you?"

She ushered him in, and they walked through the entryway and into the living room, where the woman who'd answered Milo's knock was now curled on a sofa with a bowl of popcorn, watching a movie on TV. A crime thriller with Denzel Washington, though Milo wasn't sure whether Denzel was the cop or the criminal in this one.

"Would you like something to drink, Milo? A glass of water?"

He wasn't thirsty, but he wanted something in his hands, so he said sure.

She fetched two glasses of water from the kitchen and handed one to him. They walked to the top of the stairs and down a short hallway to Cassandra's room. There were seven rooms total and, judging from the light escaping from under some of the doorways and the muffled voices and low music emanating from a few others, he guessed they were all rented out. Women only, that was the house rule, but an occasional overnight male guest was allowed, as long he only stayed one night and wasn't accompanied by any unnecessary drama.

"How are your roommates?" Milo asked.

Cassandra closed the door behind them. "Most of them are okay. One of them is a bitch, but there's always got to be one, right? Tell me what you've been up to."

She sat on the end of the bed, while he hooked the chair from her writing desk and sat down, facing her. "Spent some time in Chicago. Lived with a cowboy type for a while. Did some day labor to get by. The usual."

"Did you go to any museums there?"

"Not this trip."

"I heard that there's a museum in Chicago that has in it a World War II Nazi U-boat. They say you can look through the telescope at the people walking outside on the street."

Milo nodded. "The Museum of Science and Industry. They also have an underground coal mine with working machines and everything. I didn't get to it this time, though."

They sipped their water.

"So, I take it you need a place to stay?"

"Just for tonight. I have a job interview in one of the burbs tomorrow. Just temporary construction work, but they pay daily, under the table, I think."

"What's it been, three years?"

"Something like that. I wasn't sure I'd still find you here."

Cassandra flashed her brilliant smile again. Her pajamas had faded violins on them. "Can't beat the rent, and you know I don't like to live alone."

When Milo first met her, it was in a soup kitchen on Chicago Avenue. That was too many years ago for Milo to recall when. At the time she was living in a halfway house for abused women and working at the soup kitchen as a volunteer. He knew that under her PJs were disfiguring scars left by an angry ex.

"How long you sticking around this time?" she asked.

Milo shrugged. "Till my feet get itchy again, I guess. You know me. Living the gypsy life."

They talked for several hours, Milo artfully skipping over any details of his exploits that might link him to the Midwest Butcher's ravages. As far as Cassandra knew, he was just a harmless vagabond who blew sporadically in and out of her life.

When their conversation began to fade, he excused himself and washed in the shared, upstairs bathroom. Then he climbed naked into bed with Cassandra. They made love with the lights off. He could feel her damaged tissue rubbing against his chest and nipples, but this did not bother him.

We all have our scars to bear.

Chapter Twenty-Three

George unpacked the grocery bag from Lunds & Byerlys on the counter next to the kitchen sink: three medium beets, three medium Yukon Gold potatoes, two carrots, celery, a medium onion, a red bell pepper, vegetable broth, tomato sauce, a can of white beans, fresh bay leaves and fresh dill. Pushing the cans and seasonings off to one side, he peeled the beets, the carrots, and the onion, and left them to soak in a bowl of cold water.

He wiped his hands on a towel, then set the kitchen table.

George was no stranger to dinner parties. He'd had the Bennetts and other neighbors over several times, as well as his literary agents, faculty and students from the University of Minnesota—where he sometimes guest lectured—and the dozen or so friends he had collected over the years. Usually his parties consisted of six to eight guests, which helped keep the conversation rolling. Tonight it would just be two, but the woman seemed keen on Russian folklore, and Edmund was supposedly something of a gardening expert, so they should have plenty to discuss.

His foot felt better—at least the swelling was down—and he chose to look upon this development as a good omen.

George turned on his Bose docking station and set his iPod to shuffle. The device contained over six hours of music, American standards mostly, though some Russian folk music as well: lyrical songs that reminded him of his boyhood. He knew it wasn't the sort of music young people generally listened to, but tonight he would expand their horizons.

He'd tidied up the house, the lower level at least, except for the desk in his den, which was visible from the living room through an open door and was always messy. He liked a messy desk. Excessive order interfered with his creative process. Guests never seemed to mind. Most, he suspected, enjoyed this glimpse into his writing life.

He stepped through the living room and into the den. Perhaps they would be interested in some of the photos he had taken in the Russian Orthodox scholarly library. Yes, he would make a point of showing them. Not too many, of course, he didn't want to bore them, though the woman seemed genuinely interested in his work.

He glanced at the screen of his laptop, and a coldness crept over him.

He had lost time again this morning. Time in the mysterious fugue state, oblivious to the progressive slide of sunshine across the room. *What had it been? Four hours this time?* One minute he was sipping coffee from a porcelain mug, assembling his thoughts as he read over the last few pages of type, then—*woosh!*—he was right back in the abyss, scrabbling bestial and hedonic in a torch-lit cavern.

This time he wore the hooded robe of an acolyte, assisting in the carnage of the sacrifice to the gleeful joy of his siren of purest evil, who reached out and hugged him to her pendulous breasts where he fed like a nursing babe. The milk was sour, but he couldn't stop drinking it, and it made him swoon and plunge into disjointed visions of blood-speckled gore, screaming skulls and Cossacks atop mad, rabid steeds. A red horse reared, and the crimson rider glared down at him.

When George emerged, the clopping of the red horse's hooves still rang in his ears.

He needed a vacation, he told himself. St. Thomas or Tortola. White sands, crystalline waters, sipping a fruity drink under one of his straw hats. That was the ticket. He guessed he was too old for a shrink.

His phone rang. The landline telephone: official badge of a certified American geezer.

He answered it. "Hello?"

"Mr. Dzhurmongaliev?"

"Yes?"

"This is Denise Nils. You invited me over for dinner today?"

"Yes."

"Well, I was wondering if I might come alone."

"Without Edmund?"

"Yes. Edmund will be unable to attend tonight. His grandmother is in the hospital. It sounds like she's in pretty bad shape."

"I'm sorry to hear that."

"Yes. Well, I'd still like to come, if you don't mind. As I said, I'm very interested in your thoughts on certain Russian folktales."

"Of course. Give my best to Edmund. I hope his grandmother makes a speedy recovery."

***

Edmund couldn't take his eyes off the bedside monitor.

The bright, avocado-green tracings of the ECG waveform bumped along in slow but sharp and steady peaks. This, he knew, measured the electrical activity of the heart. He tried to figure out what the writing on it meant: GAIN, x1, LEAD II. Beneath this readout ticked along a second stream of flux, same in coloring, and similar—but not identical—to the first line. This one bore markings of red and yellow crosshairs.

The device also monitored SpO2, which he guessed had something to do with the blood's oxygen level; this line, a vibrant red, bleeped along in more pronounced peaks and valleys than the ECG lines.

Then there was the waviest of all, the yellow respiratory line, which undulated smoothly and evenly like a gentle ripple.

As long as these lines and the digital readouts beside them were active, there was hope. More hope than he felt when his sight drifted to the crumpled figure in the bed.

Maybe it was an optical illusion created by the placement of the blankets and the give of the mattress, but Grandam appeared to be going flatter, shallower, as if relinquishing substance with every rattly

137

breath. Her face was frighteningly pale. Her forehead beaded with moisture, and her silver hair curled with the wetness. Her expression, though, was the peaceful one she always wore in sleep, which leant a modicum of normalcy to all this. Perhaps the gray eyes would open again, and she would ask him about his day or tell him another story about the ancient world and the Cannibal Gardeners.

He took her hand, felt its warmth. He gazed at the monitor with its soothing, beeping lines. And became lost in reminiscence.

Chapter Twenty-Four

Denise pulled into George's driveway, heralding her approach with the dark strains of Metallica's "Until It Sleeps." Whatever the intent of its lyrics, the song, with its haunting guitar and growling chorus, always brought to her a realization of the tenuousness of our collective hold on reality, and the sinister urges that boil just below its surface. It pained her to turn off the car and end the song midway through.

For this dinner, she went modern Goth chic: brushed, wide-brimmed Panama hat, simple school-girl dress, fish-net stockings, Demonia buckled creepers, satchel purse, and a velvet choker—all in black, of course. And she wore heavy black eyeliner, with pink lipstick (for just a dab of color).

When she approached the house, George was at the door waiting.

"I'm so sorry to learn of Edmund's grandmother," George said, shaking her hand. "Has there been any word on her condition?"

"Nothing new, I'm afraid."

"Well, I hope she's alright." He ushered Denise in. "If you step this way, I was about to prepare dinner. I trust you brought your appetite."

Frank Sinatra crooned from a high-end Bose docking station.

She followed George as he limped through the spacious living room with its seldom used, bachelor furnishings; past the open door of a dimly-lit room with a cluttered writing desk inside; past a winding staircase of polished oak steps; into the kitchen, where it was sunny and roomy, and outfitted with curved, retro cabinets and counters. And an oval dining table set with china, cutlery, ringed napkins, a bowl of bread rolls, and a spray of rouge-red and honey-yellow flowers in a glass vase.

"Nice place, George."

"Thank you. To be honest, I spend most of my time here in the kitchen and in my writing room." He emptied the bowl of water and began slicing the vegetables on a swing-out cutting board. "Tell me about yourself, Denise. What do you do for a living?"

She sat on a stool at the counter, near where he was working.

"I sell things on the internet. Goth fashion stuff, mostly. On Ebay and Etsy, and my own website. I do alright. My mother left me the house when she died, and it's paid off, so that cuts out a major expense. Sometimes I take in a boarder for a little extra cash, though generally I don't live well with others."

She set her purse on the counter, opened it, and removed a copy of *Russian Wonder Tales of Baba Yaga*. She smiled at him with her eyes. "I was hoping to get you to sign my copy."

He grinned broadly. "Of course, my dear." He immediately wiped his hands, tracked down a felt-tip pen, and signed the book."How did you get interested in Russian folktales?" he said as he returned to his vegetables.

"Well, it started with the Grimm brothers." She slipped the book back into her purse. "'Hansel and Gretel' was the catalyst, as I remember. I thought the main characters were wooden, but I became fascinated with the witch. I mean, she built this fantastic edible house, solely to attract hungry children in the days of widespread famine, and when she caught them, she fattened them up and ate them. At least that was her intent with Hansel and Gretel.

"So, I started exploring other stories with characters like the witch. Not necessarily witches, but cannibal characters. From fairy tales, mythology, the classics, and so on. One day I came upon a Russian fable about this girl whose stepmother sends her off into the woods to borrow fire from a neighbor. After passing three mysterious horsemen, she comes to this house that's rotating slowly on chicken legs, and that's surrounded by a fence of human bones, and I thought, oh, my God, how twisted is that!"

"'Vasilisa the Beautiful,'" George said.

"Yes. Well, you know the story, of course. But when Baba Yaga rode in on a whirlwind in her flying mortar, with her razor teeth of iron and her one leg of exposed bone, she struck me as such an embodiment of evil. I mean, she's a demigod, right? Who kills on a whim and is eager to devour the flesh of her victims? She completely blew my mind."

George motioned toward her with a peeled potato. "Well, in that tale, Baba Yaga helps the young girl, sending her back home unscathed with hot coals for her fire."

"Burning coals in a human skull, as I recall." Denise's eyes widened and her cheeks flushed with color. "And only after threatening Vasilisa and making her perform tasks that would have been impossible if the girl hadn't possessed a haunted doll that did the chores for her. And don't forget the disembodied hands that followed her every move when Baba Yaga left her alone. How frightening is that? Being trailed around all the time by floating hands?" Denise contorted her face, as if she'd just smelled something awful. "And, let's face it, it made no difference to Baba Yaga whether or not the girl succeeded in her challenge. She would have been just as happy to butcher Vasilisa as to allow her to live. Probably happier."

George smiled at her display of enthusiasm. "Well, you're right, of course. Some of the more recent accounts paint Baba Yaga in a nobler light. In literature, there's always a movement underway to civilize these stories and make them more palatable for modern readers. Has been for years. A sort of evolution to defang the tales, or at least smooth over their rough edges. The Grimm brothers did that themselves in subsequent versions of their stories."

"To appease the masses, I suppose. But personally I find the original, darker versions much more interesting," Denise said thoughtfully, fingering her choker.

"Judging from the success of Walt Disney, I'd say toning them down is a smart marketing move." He turned on the stove and began sautéing the vegetables in a Dutch oven.

"But don't you find we learn more about ourselves by peeking into dark corners?"

"Sometimes. Sometimes what we see in those shadows are horrors beyond anything we imagined."

"That depends on the limits of the viewer's imagination."

From the living room, the stereo played Dean Martin. "Ain't That a Kick in the Head."

After the other veggies had cooked a while, George added the beans, the vegetable stock, and six cups of water. He minced the dill and added that, along with the bay leaves and some minced garlic from a jar. He splashed in a little vinegar, and ground pepper from a mill.

They made light conversation while he worked, remarking on the weather and the colorful approach of autumn, on the gathering of the geese for their upcoming flight south, and on the sail boats and motor boats that flocked Lake Minnetonka at season's end.

He sprayed cleaner on the cutting board, wiped it down and folded it away. Denise could see where the beets had stained his hands red.

They talked about Edmund's gardening skills. George, at one point, gestured out the window to the Bennett's backyard and Denise walked over and looked. The flowers shined full and lush in the patio light.

"Aren't they beautiful?" George said.

Denise agreed they were.

As the borscht cooked, they discussed the source materials George used in the Baba Yaga book Denise had in her purse, the difficulties of marrying sometimes wildly dissimilar versions of the same story, and finding English words that aligned with not just the meaning but the spirit of the original Russian. Of the liberties all translators took in their work.

When the soup was ready, George brought the pot and a ladle to the table. He served up two bowls, topping them off with dollops of sour cream. He poured two glasses of wine. Sauvignon Blanc.

The steamy soup was blood red and had a wonderful, slightly bitter flavor.

"My mother told me that in the old country they sometimes used duck's blood in their borscht," George said.

"I'd try it that way," Denise replied.

As they spooned down the borscht, the conversation shifted to George's next book, which Denise was delighted to learn was also about Baba Yaga.

"This one goes to her very beginnings," George said, "before the fables about her. Back to when she was worshiped by cults that held human sacrifices and cannibal rituals in her honor. Ghoulish cabals on par with the ancient Aztecs."

He told her the story of the documents unearthed in the Russian Orthodox library and how he came to study them with the blessings of the highest church officials. Of the shocking details these records revealed.

"That's fantastic," she said, gaping, a drop of borscht on the pink sheen of her lower lip.

"After dinner, I'll show you some photos from the Orthodox library. Some of these chronicles were replicas of lead plates dating back before 800 CE. Some were scrolls. It was quite a coup, getting access to these writings."

He was quiet for a while. Then he said, "Immersing myself in these scripts has had an unsettling effect on me, I'm afraid. Most unsettling."

George went still, a spoonful of borscht suspended in midair, his gaze focused on something only he could see.

Denise reached across the table and touched his sleeve. "Are you alright?"

The liveliness had left his demeanor. He looked across at her, his prosthetic eye lagging a bit. The rest of him remained still. Finally, he said, "Physically, yes. Mentally ... I'm not so sure."

"Writing this book has really taken a toll on you, hasn't it?"

"Yes. It's like these ancient texts have some kind of power over me." His face turned, and the glass eye now perfectly matched the direction the real one pointed. "They put me in a trance, unlike anything I've ever experienced before."

"Maybe you should take a break from it."

"I can't. Not now. It's nearly completed."

They finished their meal in silence, then George led her through the dark living room to his writing den. He turned on the desk lamp. A large throw rug, aquamarine and hand-hooked, filled the center of the floor. Cramped bookshelves lined the walls. George sat down in the desk's chair, tapped the keyboard, and the Toshiba came to life. He selected a cloud drive from his bookmarks, entered a password, and opened a file.

The first photographs were of uneven rectangles of lead. One plate featured crude etchings of Baba Yaga, imagined as a terrifying demon, jagged teeth crunching on someone's severed femur.

"This one came from a cavern in Pskov. See these indents at the edges?" He moved his finger along the image. "At one time, this tablet was part of a book, held together by leather ties, which decomposed over time. Some of the other pages of the book are here. A few are just fragments."

He moved through several more tablets, before coming to the scrolls.

"Now some of these parchments were so brittle, I could only unroll them in sections, as you can see here." He flipped through the images until he came to a flattened scroll. "Now this is interesting. This parchment is from a people called the Gostrados, who lived in the Biebrza Marshes in what is now Suwalki, Poland. Look how detailed these illustrations are of their sacrificial ceremonies. The different clerics, the blades, which appear to be made of obsidian. One thing especially noteworthy about this piece is that there is no mention of Baba Yaga in it, though she appears in later Gostrado texts, which may mean that this cult was cannibal *before* it adopted her as its icon."

Denise looked with awe at the hooded caricatures. "These images are mesmerizing."

Suddenly she felt ill at ease. She looked around in the shadows of the room. "George, is someone else here?"

He looked up from the computer screen. "Not that I know of."

She held up a hand for him to be quiet, her head cocked to one side under the wide brim of her Panama hat. She squinched her eyes in concentration, listening intently over Bobby Darin's velvety voice singing, "Beyond the Sea."

Then she turned to George and whispered, "I think there's someone in your living room."

Chapter Twenty-Five

The madman grimaced as the floorboard gave out a groan. In the next room, the conversation went silent for a moment, followed by whispering.

He set down his canvas tote and removed the butcher knife he had, just that afternoon, honed to a razor edge. The heft of the knife felt good in his hand. He gripped the handle tightly as he moved through the dark toward the open doorway.

They stared at him as he stepped through the threshold, startled in the way one can only be by the sudden upturning of all reality.

"Who are you?" the terror-stricken author Yegor Dzhurmongaliev demanded.

"Who am I? Why I am the Midwest Butcher, bringer of death, at your service."

A stunned silence gripped the room.

"What do you want?" the old boy demanded at last, rising shakily from his chair.

"Sit down!" Milo barked. "You're going to answer some questions for me, or I promise you your obstinance will be greatly regretted."

The woman's shock melted to a watchful amazement.

"Where does she come from?" Milo said.

Yegor glanced uncertainly at the woman in the room. "Where does who come from?"

"Who? Who? Who do you think, you old fool. The Russian witch, the demon with the iron teeth!"

"Baba Yaga?"

He lunged the blade menacingly. "Don't pretend you're unaware of who or what she is. Now tell me, where does she come from?"

"Well," the old boy said, struggling with the question, "as near as I can tell, she comes from the forests and swamps of Poland and Belarus. From tribes called the Gostrados, the Azhbaguls and the Zhodislavas, who worshiped her as a god."

Milo pondered this for a moment. "Who are the horsemen?"

The old boy looked at the woman, as if she might help him come up with an answer. "Uh, you mean the white, the red and the black Cossacks from 'Vasilisa the Beautiful?'"

"Yes."

"Watchmen, perhaps. They serve Baba Yaga, that's clear from all the source materials. But in what capacity, I'm not sure anyone knows for certain."

"I thought you knew all about her!"

Yegor stared at the tip of the knife. "I know as much as anyone alive."

"Then tell me this...." Milo took another a sinister step toward the old boy. "Why is she under my skin? Why does she ride me like she does? Why does she compel me to do things for her?"

"What does she compel you to do?"

"Don't pretend you don't know. You serve her, too, don't you?'

For a minute, Yegor looked dumbfounded. Then he said, "I think maybe yes."

Milo brought the blade closer, almost touching the old boy's chin.

The woman, who Milo had all but forgotten, chose this moment to attack.

She grabbed the wrist of his knife hand, turned, and pulled him to her back. She leaned forward and threw him over her shoulder to the ground. The air rushed out of him. The butcher knife spun across the floor. Blinking his eyes against waves of swarming blackness, he rose awkwardly to one elbow, got a leg under himself, and tottered to his feet, gasping for air.

If it had just been the woman, she might have escaped. But the old boy slowed her down, as they fumbled toward the doorway. Milo felt the transformation beginning within him: the violent upsurge of energy as his goddess scratched her way from his stomach into his throat. He felt her rip through his trachea and his larynx. She filled his mouth, stretching it until his jaw unhinged to dangle loosely on his chest.

She crawled from the ragged hole in his burst face, shaking her hips like an exotic dancer until his gory sheath slid down her thighs, and she stepped, bony leg leading, onto the patterned, aquamarine rug.

Chapter Twenty-Six

D enise froze—not in terror but in awe.

She stared into the yellow, hatred-filled eyes of Baba Yaga. Into the warty, creased face; the bloated nose; the malicious, iron-toothed grin. Steam rose from the figure's shoulders and leaden hair. In one hand, Baba Yaga held tight to an enormous pestle, cocking it back like a club, ready to strike.

The patched furrows of her peasant dress rasped as she took a jolting step forward.

Behind her, the madman was somehow pulling himself together. Flecked gore sucked back into his body like a film run in reverse. The wrenched-back head slapped forward, settling unevenly on his ripped-open jaw. His burst and stretched flesh squirmed and worked itself back into place.

He struggled to his feet and fetched the butcher blade from where it had settled

George screamed. The terrible, wailing cry filled the room. He sank in his chair, and began convulsing from the hips and stomach. He crashed to the floor in a full-blown seizure, the chair falling over backward.

Denise tried to move toward him but couldn't. She felt suddenly disembodied, witnessing the horrors unfolding around her from some distant, dreamlike perspective.

Baba Yaga waved long, dirty fingernails dismissively at Denise, and turned instead toward George, the goddess' unofficial biographer.

Now fear hammered in Denise's heart, not for her but for George, who twitched helplessly on the floor.

"Bony leg," she said. "Goddess of the Gostrados, the Azhbaguls and the Zhodislavas. Great Baba Yaga, choose me." The words escaped her numb lips before she had a chance to weight their consequences. But the surge of resolve was real. "Choose me."

The witch's head snapped in her direction. The hulking form went motionless, as if all time had stopped. Baba Yaga studied Denise, yellow eyes fraught with curiosity. She lumbered over to her, sniffed, bared teeth. Between the iron razors in her mouth were trapped shreds of a former repast. Her breath was thick with the smell of decay.

"Please," Denise whispered. "Take me."

Baba Yaga spun and brought the pestle down on the head of the madman at her rear with such force that it caved his forehead and brought a wash of blood pouring over his startled face below. Denise watched as the Midwest Butcher, bringer of death to countless innocents, tasted of it himself. His disjointed body collapsed to the floor.

Turning back to Denise, the goddess leaned in and winked one yellow eye. The bloody pestle vanished into her clothing. She took Denise's head in her hands.

Denise surrendered to the touch.

Evil exploded within her, from her deepest hollows. It howled in her bones and roared through her veins. Treachery, cunning, lust, avarice, greed, wrath, every shade of wickedness and corruption roiled in a bubbling, white-hot ball through her blood, through her muscles, up her spinal cord and down every neuron to every nerve ending in her body, slamming into her brain like a rocket.

Her personality came undone; her thoughts rearranged themselves to make room for this vile, new temperament. This modified version of herself as a permanent plus-one.

She felt her jaw yank open, tear free of its hinges, felt her throat widen to an impossible width. Felt the monster snake inside her, and settle in.

Denise, possessed of a strength and power that radiated down her arms and hummed in her belly, turned to the dead, prone figure of Milo Castellanos, and lifted it over one shoulder.

***

George awoke on the floor. His heart was still racing. He looked around for Denise, for Baba Yaga, for the madman who had broken into his house, but there was no sign of any of them. He sat up, bracing himself as lightheadedness buffeted him. When the room stopped spinning, he climbed shakily to his feet.

He couldn't have just imagined all of this. Could he?

His old friend, the pseudogout, made a throbbing appearance as he wended his way into the darkened living room. He peered out the doorway. Denise's devil-red sports car was gone.

The light was still on in the kitchen. He moved out there, hoping to find a note or some other sign of what had happened after he'd blacked out. The Dutch oven was still on the table. Automatically, he put the lid on it to cover the borscht and carried it to the fridge. The leftover rolls he put into a baggy and was about to refrigerate them when something caught his eye.

On the front burner of the stove was one of his frying pans. *What is that doing there?* He hadn't used it in preparing dinner. He picked it up by the handle and examined it closely. It had been used to fry something.

Some kind of meat.

T he visitation was a sparse affair, not like Pamela Bates' had been. Grandam had few friends, and most of them lived in southern cities far away and were too frail to travel, so they opted instead to send cards and flowers. The attendees were almost wholly friends of Edmund's: people he went to school with, people from work, neighbors, the Bennetts. Even Rudy showed up, though he looked strangely unfamiliar, having swapped his chauffer's getup for a regular suit and tie. The smattering of guests signed the guest book, offered their condolences, and moved on with their lives.

Only Taylin stayed with Edmund the whole day.

Grandam was cremated and displayed in a rosewood urn, alongside framed photographs taken of her during celebrations.

Denise didn't come at all, which Edmund found odd, given her penchant for all things funereal. In coming days he would call her but would get no answer. Finally, he gave up trying. For whatever reason, she had ghosted him. He let her go. But he kept her picture from the Forlorn Flesh Fetishist on a jump drive. Sometimes he would look at it and feel the old heat again.

Taylin helped him move his few things from Grandam's apartment to the Bennett's gardener cottage. Of Grandam's possessions, he kept some of the utilitarian items: the Tiffany lamp from the living room, her rocking chair, the noisy old coffee maker, a few utensils. He also kept the crocodile-hide suitcase that was hidden under her bed. The one she teased him about.

And, of course, he kept the impossibly perfect plants in their macramé slings and painted clay pots: the ferns, the orchids, the ponytail palms, the devil's ivy, the jade and the zebra plants. He continued to nourish these with loving care and they brought a familiar brightness to his new home.

He bought a used Honda Rebel 300 motorcycle to get around on and the Bennetts let him keep it in the corner of the garage. It was economical and good for transportation on snowless days, spring through fall. When winter came, he would have to make other arrangements. The nearest bus stop was nine miles away, so maybe Rudy could chauffer him that far, or maybe he could get a lift from a neighbor headed off to work.

Some days, he could even hitch a ride all the way to Harbo's Garden Center in a certain white sedan with a steering wheel shaped like a heart, and butterflies on the floor mats the color of grape jelly.

After he moved in, he saw little of George Dzhurmongaliev. The ancient writer ceased visiting the Bennetts, and when Edmund knocked on George's door and offered his services as a gardener, the old fellow had developed a distant, washed-out look. His wrinkles ran deeper, and his skin had a chalky texture. The only thing that remained vibrant in George's face was the green of his glass eye. He politely declined Edmund's offer and cut short the visit.

On lonely nights in the quiet of the gardener's cottage, Edmund missed Grandam's company. He missed her humor and heartfelt advice. He missed her stories about the Kai-Tangata and how they became the Cannibal Gardeners. Sometimes when he felt down this way, he would watch a program on the nostalgia channel, *Mannix* or *The Man from U.N.C.L.E.* Sometimes he would finger her things: the heart-shaped pendant he had bought for her years ago on her birthday, the heirloom brooch her mother had given her that she only wore on special occasions, and the worn, crocodile suitcase, though he usually only opened it when he felt really sad and alone.

He quit going on the dark web. He no longer felt drawn to its gloomy shores.

That didn't mean he'd forsaken his connection to his ancestry. It was still a part of him. We are, after all, what we are: stardust and memories and the tailings of ghosts that haunt us from before we were born. But it was a part of him he now chose, by and large, to tuck away.

Most days he was okay with that. Outside his window, in the Bennett's garden, petals bloomed and roots sank deep, and the sun and the rain were always there to work their magic upon the land. And maybe that was all he really needed.

That and the touch of warm flesh when he pressed his body against Taylin's, and smelled the faint scent of her orange perfume.

When he wanted to get back in touch with that other side of himself, he always had the crocodile suitcase's contents.

Inside it, carefully padded and wrapped in old newspapers, were a baker's dozen—handed down from generation to generation, he supposed—thirteen genuine shrunken heads.

He liked to think they were Koroghori warriors, the ancient enemies of the Kai-Tangata. But he couldn't be sure. Grandam had never mentioned having these heads. He had only discovered them when going through her things for the move.

When he unwrapped them, he searched their tanned, shriveled faces for some insight into the big questions he knew even Grandam couldn't answer. Questions like: What is the purpose of life? Why must we suffer through hardship, great losses, and the erosion of our dreams? What truth lies beyond the veil of darkness? And, Why must we pay such a dear toll to glimpse it?

But the mouths of the shrunken heads were sewn shut, and their somber faces betrayed no secrets.

> Acknowledgments

Baba Yaga is a genuine character from Russian folklore, every bit as frightening as she is portrayed in this book. However, as far as I know, she has never been connected to an ancient cannibal cult (though such cults did indeed exist) and she has never been accused of possessing anyone, though, for a demon, that's hardly beyond the realm of possibility.

Also, the origin of the Cannibal Gardeners of New Guinea (but not the Cannibal Gardeners themselves) was a literary fabrication. Joseph Campbell, the esteemed author of many books on mythology and comparative religion, wrote about the Cannibal Gardeners in *The Masks of God*.

Thanks to Jennifer Thompson for proofreading and to Danita Mayer for her editing, kind words and encouragement. I also thank my wife, Debbie, for her support, and for letting me be myself and accepting all the weirdness that entails.

If you enjoyed *The Cannibal Gardener*, consider recommending it to your friends and family on social media. Also, reader reviews are the lifeblood of modern publishing, and posting a brief review on Amazon, Goodreads or your favorite readers' blog would help a struggling author immeasurably.

For updates on my work and for further readings on dark fiction, check out my website at: www.joepawlowskiauthor.com. You can follow me on Facebook @ Joe Pawlowski, Author or on Instagram @ joepawlowskiauthor.

Let the Terror Continue

OTHER BOOKS BY JOE PAWLOWSKI

The Watchful Dead

A 12-year-old boy housebound all his life, a conjure woman who speaks to the dead, an evil slave trader driven ruthless by greed and a war hero whose greatest battles take place in his own mind: all are about to have their lives shaken to the core by powerful forces from beyond the grave.

Readers are calling it "a ride right off the bat" and "nicely written, with a lyrical quality that kept me turning virtual pages," and the author "possesses the talents of a classic great writer."

The Horror Review says *The Watchful Dead* is "a gutsy, ambitious, skillful exploration of cosmic/epic dark fantasy."

Available from Amazon in paperback and ebook. Free on Kindle Unlimited.

Dark House of Dreams

In a city overrun by ghosts, fear lurks around every corner.

Add a murder plot, a devastating earthquake, a missing mother, a gang of outrageous villains, and a young boy tormented by demons both real and imagined, and you have an epic quest through the hidden places of monsters and gods.

Readers say it's a "well-written and creepy" journey that begins with a secret revealed in a charnel cave and ends with a hard-earned lesson learned in a *Dark House of Dreams*.

Available from Amazon in paperback and ebook. Free on Kindle Unlimited.

The Vermilion Book of the Macabre.

From author of *The Cannibal Gardener* and *Dark House of Dreams* comes this highly anticipated collection of 16 spellbinding tales of supernatural suspense.

Readers marvel call it "a blood-chilling collection" and say of Pawlowski "he paints his dark tales so realistically you will have nightmares."

Available from Amazon in paperback and ebook. Free on Kindle Unlimited.

Made in the USA
Monee, IL
13 June 2021